Enjoy all of these American Girl Mysteries®:

and many more!

— A *Marie-Grace* MYSTERY —

THE HAUNTED
OPERA

by Sarah Masters Buckey

Published by American Girl Publishing
Copyright © 2013 by American Girl

Questions or comments? Call 1-800-845-0005,
visit **americangirl.com**, or write to Customer Service,
American Girl, 8400 Fairway Place, Middleton, WI 53562-0497.

Printed in China
13 14 15 16 17 18 LEO 10 9 8 7 6 5 4 3 2 1

This book is a work of fiction. Any similarity to real persons, living or dead,
is coincidental and not intended by American Girl. References to real events,
people, or places are used fictitiously. Other names, characters, places, and
incidents are the products of imagination.

PICTURE CREDITS
The following individuals and organizations have generously
given permission to reprint illustrations contained in "Looking Back":
pp. 162–163—*French Opera House* by Boyd Cruise (detail), collection of
Mr. Joseph H. Epstein, Jr.; University of Michigan Museum of Art, Bequest of
Henry C. Lewis, 1895.24, detail (portrait of Anna Thillon); courtesy, American
Antiquarian Society (playbill); pp. 164–165—Photograph courtesy of the
Metropolitan Opera Archives (opera performance); © Bibliothèque nationale
de France (actors in *The Crown Diamonds*); The Historic New Orleans Collection,
accession no. 1963.7 (St. Charles Theater); pp. 166–167—The Historic
New Orleans Collection, accession no. 1951.74i-v (opera audience);
Eda Kuhn Loeb Music Library of the Harvard College Library (opera program);
Wisconsin Historial Society, WHS-1965.97.14 (white gloves); pp. 168–169—artist:
Phil Rodeghiero, photo by Gene Salecker (steamboat fire); Letter from Vilet Lester
to Patsey Patterson, 1857, Joseph Allred Papers, David M. Rubinstein Rare Book
& Manuscript Library, Duke University; © Corbis (New Orleans graveyard).

Illustrations by Sergio Giovine

Cataloging-in-Publication data
available from the Library of Congress

For Chrissie

In 1854, many people in New Orleans had French names and spoke French as well as English. You'll see some French words and names in this book. Look in the glossary on page 170 for help in pronouncing them.

TABLE OF CONTENTS

1

SPIES BACKSTAGE

As the horse-drawn carriage splashed along the rainy streets of New Orleans, Marie-Grace looked out toward the Mississippi River. "Where is the ship you're going to visit, Papa?"

"Look, you can see it there," said her father, Dr. Thaddeus Gardner. He pointed toward a ship with faded blue paint that was docked along the river. "It's called the *Georgia*."

"Whoa!" the driver, Mr. Fitzgerald, said to his horse. On this chilly February day, the horse was full of energy. It snorted impatiently as Papa picked up his medical bag and stepped from the carriage.

"The captain says many passengers are sick, so I'll be aboard the ship for quite some time," Papa said. "But Mr. Fitzgerald will take you to the

Royal Music Hall." He smiled at Marie-Grace. "I hope you and your aunt have a good time."

"We will, Papa!" said Marie-Grace. She waved good-bye, and the horse started off again. Marie-Grace felt a damp breeze on her face as she watched the familiar sights of the city. Store owners were opening their shuttered shops, women were heading to the market with baskets over their arms, and street vendors were calling out, "Fresh fruit!"

It was Saturday—Marie-Grace's favorite day of the week. On Saturday mornings, she and her best friend, Cécile, studied singing at the Royal Music Hall. Their teacher was *Madame* Océane, the kind and talented young opera singer who had recently married Marie-Grace's Uncle Luc.

Marie-Grace rarely got to see her aunt except during their Saturday lessons, because Aunt Océane and Uncle Luc lived on the other side of the city. This Saturday, however, Uncle Luc, a steamboat pilot, was away on a voyage, so Aunt Océane and Marie-Grace were going to spend the whole afternoon together.

While the carriage rumbled along, Marie-Grace imagined the afternoon ahead. *Aunt Océane and I will have tea and cookies first*, she decided. *Then we can take a walk through the city and look at shop windows.*

Marie-Grace sometimes saw other girls strolling by shop windows, laughing and talking with their mothers. Her own mother and her baby brother had died when she was five, and now she lived only with Papa. Marie-Grace loved her father very much, but he was a busy doctor. He would never want to spend an afternoon strolling and shopping in town. *It will be so nice to spend time with Aunt Océane*, Marie-Grace thought happily as the carriage turned onto a wide avenue.

They passed a fancy hotel and a brick post office, and then they reached the Royal Music Hall, an impressive building with tall columns. It was set across from an old church and a cemetery surrounded by a tall iron fence.

Mr. Fitzgerald slowed the carriage to a halt. As Marie-Grace climbed down, her feet sank into a cold puddle. But she hardly noticed. She was looking at a large broadside that had been posted in front of the Royal Music Hall:

Foxcroft's London Opera Company

Presents

THE CROWN DIAMONDS

Starring

MISS SYLVIA BELL

"The Belle of London"

and

MR. ROBERTO DICARLO

Opens Thursday

The Crown Diamonds! thought Marie-Grace. Even the name sounded exciting.

She wasn't surprised to see people already lined up in front of the Royal Music Hall, waiting to buy tickets. Everyone in New Orleans—young and old, rich and poor—loved opera. The arrival of a new opera company from London was an important event. The performances would be written about in newspapers and talked about everywhere. Some of the wealthiest girls at Marie-Grace's school, St. Teresa's Academy, went to the theater almost every week, and they liked to brag about all the operas they'd seen.

Marie-Grace had been to only a few operas. But whenever Papa had taken her to a show, she'd soaked in everything—the action-filled stories, the gorgeous costumes, the fancy scenery, and, best of all, the beautiful music.

Maybe we can see this new opera! she thought.

Papa did not allow her to attend operas on school nights, but this show had arrived at a perfect time. The roof at St. Teresa's Academy had been leaking and was being replaced, so there would be no school next week. *I'll ask Papa if we can get tickets for opening night.*

She ran up the flight of marble steps in front of the building. She passed the ticket box and entered the spacious lobby of the Royal Music Hall. In front of her, the hallway stretched to the back of the building. To her right, a wide staircase led to the musicians' studios on the upper floors. To her left, four sets of double doors arranged in a half circle led to the grand theater.

The doors to the theater were closed, but Marie-Grace could hear the muffled sound of a chorus singing. She walked toward the theater, trying to catch every note. Suddenly, a familiar voice called from across the lobby, *"Bonjour, Marie-Grace! You're early!"*

Marie-Grace turned and saw Cécile being escorted into the music hall by her young maid, who was holding an umbrella over both of them. The maid said good-bye, and Cécile quickly crossed the lobby. She was wearing a rose-colored dress trimmed with lace that set off her brown skin and hazel eyes.

"Bonjour, Cécile!" Marie-Grace greeted her friend in French. Like many people in New Orleans, Cécile spoke both French and English and often switched back and forth between the languages. "Listen—they must be practicing for the new show!"

The chorus reached a high note, and then the sound seemed to fade. Cécile said, "Let's go into the theater so we can hear them better."

Marie-Grace nodded enthusiastically. She was often shy when she was by herself, but Cécile always had good ideas for adventures. *I'm so glad she's here*, thought Marie-Grace.

The two girls had met at the Royal Music Hall more than a year ago. In some ways, it had been unlikely that they ever would have become friends. Marie-Grace was white, and her widower father had little time to socialize. Cécile was a free girl of color, and her prosperous family usually socialized with other free people of color. But Marie-Grace and Cécile shared a love of music, theater—and adventures.

Cécile and Marie-Grace pushed against the doors, but they were locked.

"I know! If we go the back way, we could watch from behind the stage," suggested Cécile, a glint of mischief in her eyes.

Both girls had been backstage with Aunt Océane, and they knew that the back stairs were supposed to be for people in the show. But as Marie-Grace stood by the locked entrance doors, she could catch only tantalizing bits of the music. She desperately wanted to hear more. Her eyes met Cécile's. "Let's try it."

The girls hurried along the central hallway to the building's rear entrance. Usually Louis, an elderly doorman, guarded this entrance. Today, however, he was nowhere in sight. Marie-Grace and Cécile went up the steps to the backstage area.

The music sounded closer as they walked quickly along a hall lined with doors. They passed an office and several dressing rooms. A sign on one dressing room door said "Mr. Roberto DiCarlo." Another sign read "Mr. Thomas Taylor." Just across the hall, a large sign in fancy script proclaimed "Miss Sylvia Bell."

"*Mademoiselle* Bell must be the prima donna," Cécile said in a low voice.

"Yes, she's the star of the opera," Marie-Grace whispered back.

The girls entered the theater's greenroom, a large room where the cast and crew members gathered to relax. Several men in work clothes were drinking coffee at the long table in the center of the room. As Marie-Grace walked by, she heard one man say, "I hope *The Crown Diamonds* goes better this time than it did the last time."

"*Mon Dieu,* I still remember that," another man replied, shaking his head. "That was terrible."

What happened last time? Marie-Grace wondered as she followed Cécile through the greenroom and down a short set of stairs to the back of the stage.

The girls made their way through ropes that hung from pulleys, like vines dangling from trees. Finally, they reached the heavy red velvet stage curtain. The glorious music was getting louder now.

Peeking from behind the curtain, Marie-Grace saw the backs of the chorus members just a few yards away. Beyond the chorus, the elegant theater's red velvet seats were empty, and the gold-painted balconies and enormous crystal chandelier were all in shadow.

But light was shining on the stage, where a pianist accompanied the chorus's rehearsal. A tall, white-haired man directed the singers. The director was dressed in a formal black suit, and he was swinging his baton in time to the music. Marie-Grace could see his stern face clearly. She tried to shrink behind the curtain so that he wouldn't see her.

From her hiding place, Marie-Grace could hear the music perfectly. It was so powerful that the stage seemed to tremble. But suddenly the director threw down his baton, and the music broke off abruptly. "No, no!" he shouted at the chorus. "You are a disgrace—have you never sung before?"

Marie-Grace's eyes widened in surprise. The chorus members shuffled their music nervously. "This is our first rehearsal, Mr. Foxcroft," some-one protested.

"That's no excuse!" he thundered. "I'm paying you to sing, and you sound like howling cats!"

No one said a word.

Cécile turned to Marie-Grace. "I thought it

sounded wonderful!" Her voice was barely above a whisper, but it echoed on the silent stage.

The director turned. "What are you doing back there?" he roared, pointing a white-gloved hand at the girls. "Do you dare to spy on my rehearsal?"

Oh no! thought Marie-Grace. She quickly stepped back, and her foot caught on one of the dangling ropes. She almost fell, but Cécile steadied her just in time. Mr. Foxcroft was striding toward them, and he looked furious.

"Allons-y!" Cécile whispered, tugging Marie-Grace's arm. "Let's go!"

The girls turned and rushed through the maze of ropes to the greenroom. They ran past the dressing rooms and back to the main floor. When they reached the lobby, Marie-Grace glanced at the double doors leading to the theater, half afraid that Mr. Foxcroft would be standing there, scowling at them. But the doors were still closed. The girls raced across the lobby and up the wide steps toward the studios.

"Gracious sakes! He almost caught us!"

Marie-Grace said breathlessly when they reached the safety of the second floor.

"Yes! And did you see how mad he looked?" Cécile imitated the director's fierce glare. Her expression was so perfect that Marie-Grace giggled.

Cécile giggled, too. Then, relieved by their escape, both girls started laughing. Marie-Grace flung open the door to her Aunt Océane's music studio. But her aunt wasn't sitting at her usual place in front of the grand piano. Instead, Marie-Grace heard the clatter of a teacup from behind the painted screen that separated her aunt's sitting area from the music area. Still laughing uproariously, she and Cécile ran around the screen.

"Aunt Océane—" Marie-Grace began. Then she stopped short. Her aunt was not alone. She was drinking tea with a small, plump woman in an expensive-looking dress. Aunt Océane's guest had a pink and white complexion, a slight double chin, and blonde hair arranged in stylish ringlets.

Aunt Océane raised her eyebrows, as if in warning. Then in her soft French accent she said, "Marie-Grace, Cécile, I would like you to meet Miss Bell, who has come all the way from England. She'll be playing Queen Catarina, the leading role in *The Crown Diamonds*."

A real opera star, right here! Marie-Grace realized. As she made a deep curtsy, her heart clanged with excitement.

"I'm delighted to meet you," said Miss Bell in a crisp British accent. She gave the girls a gracious nod.

Aunt Océane told them that she and Miss Bell had met years ago, when they'd both sung in an opera in Paris.

"It's been a long time—that was my first solo role!" Miss Bell said, and her laughter echoed in the room like the ringing of a silver bell. "It's good to see you again, Océane," she added. "We've had so many troubles on this trip, but finding you here is a happy surprise. You will be perfect for Henrietta's role!"

"Thank you," said Aunt Océane, blushing. She

turned to the girls and explained that Henrietta had been a lead singer with Mr. Foxcroft's touring opera company. When the company had left England a few weeks ago, they had planned to perform in Cuba before coming to New Orleans to begin their American tour.

"None of us had crossed the Atlantic Ocean before, and we were all quite excited about our American debut!" said Miss Bell.

But, Miss Bell continued, during the trip Henrietta had come down with a fever. By the time they had arrived in Cuba, the singer had lost her voice and become weak, and other members of the cast were ill, too. Mr. Foxcroft had canceled their performance and arranged for Henrietta to recover in Cuba. Henrietta's sister, who'd been her understudy, had insisted on staying with her.

Now the company needed a local singer to replace Henrietta, and Aunt Océane had been chosen for the role. She would also be Miss Bell's understudy.

Cécile looked curious. "What's an understudy?"

Miss Bell explained that an understudy was an actor who practiced another actor's role. "So if, for any reason, I cannot sing the role of Queen Catarina, Madame Océane will take my place, and a member of the chorus will step in to take Madame Océane's role."

Miss Bell pursed her lips. "I've heard that there were—er—some problems the last time *The Crown Diamonds* was performed here, but I'm sure nothing will go wrong this time." She gave a little nervous laugh.

"No indeed," Aunt Océane agreed quickly.

Marie-Grace and Cécile exchanged a glance. Marie-Grace wondered, *What **did** happen last time?*

"Océane, we have much to do before opening on Thursday, and we'll be working long hours," Miss Bell said. "I'm staying at the hotel down the street. Is your home close by?"

"Not really," Aunt Océane admitted. "But my husband is away, so I can sleep here this week," she added, patting the velvet sofa they were sitting on. "I'll be able to work as late as

I need to." Aunt Océane smiled. "I'm very grateful for this role, Miss Bell. I promise I shall not disappoint you."

They all looked up as a knock sounded at the door. A tall, sturdy woman with a square jaw and brown hair pulled into a tight bun marched into the studio. "Ma'am, I'm sorry to disturb you," she told Miss Bell. "The seamstress would like to see you about your costume—the one that was ruined on the voyage."

"Thank you, Greta," said Miss Bell.

She turned back to Aunt Océane. "Not only did most of us become ill during the voyage, but our trunks got wet, too. My best costume was soaked." She sighed dramatically. "I don't know what I'd do without my maid Greta to help me." The prima donna stood up, and promising to return later, she hurried away.

As soon as the door closed behind Miss Bell, Aunt Océane turned to the girls. "I can hardly believe it!" she said, sounding stunned. "For so long, I've dreamed of having a role like this. And now my dream has come true!"

Then she put her hand on Marie-Grace's shoulder. "But I'm sorry, my dear niece. I won't be able to enjoy this afternoon with you. After you and Cécile have your lessons, I'll need to start practicing my part."

"I understand," said Marie-Grace, trying to hide her disappointment.

Conversation swirled around her for a few moments as Aunt Océane and Cécile talked about the upcoming opera. Aunt Océane was describing a costume that Ida, the seamstress at the Royal Music Hall, was making for her, when Marie-Grace had an idea.

"Aunt Océane," she burst out, "I don't have school next week! If you'd like, I could stay here with you and help you."

"I could certainly use your help during rehearsals," Aunt Océane agreed. "But you must ask your father first."

"I wish I didn't have lessons next week so I could help too," Cécile exclaimed. Then she brightened. "I know! I'll ask *Maman* if I can come in the afternoons, after my lessons are done."

Marie-Grace imagined how exciting it would be to stay with Aunt Océane until the opera opened. Cécile would visit, too, and every day would be filled with music.

I hope Papa says yes!

2
THE QUEEN

To Marie-Grace's great relief, her father agreed to her plan.

"So many of the passengers aboard the *Georgia* are ill that I'll be needed there much of the week," Papa said that evening. "So perhaps it would be a good idea if you stayed with your aunt for the next few days."

After church on Sunday, Papa hired Mr. Fitzgerald's carriage and took Marie-Grace to the Royal Music Hall. The air smelled damp, but it wasn't raining yet, and the streets were crowded with people. Wealthy families, many accompanied by servants or slaves, were strolling along the *banquettes*, the wooden sidewalks that lined the streets.

Outside the Royal Music Hall, more people

were lined up to buy tickets for *The Crown Diamonds*. Papa promised that he would get tickets for opening night.

I'll get to see Aunt Océane perform, thought Marie-Grace with a rush of joy.

After saying good-bye to her father, she avoided the crowds by slipping around to the back door of the music hall. Louis, the doorman, greeted her cheerfully. He asked about her dog, Argos, who usually accompanied her when she walked to the music hall.

"Argos is fine, but I had to leave him at home with our housekeeper," said Marie-Grace. She showed him the satchel of clothes she was carrying. "I'm staying here for a few days to help my aunt."

"Ah, *bien*, I'm sure she's happy to have your help," said Louis. He lowered his voice. "But I warn you, Mr. Foxcroft is not happy with anyone today. If I were you, I'd stay out of his way."

Marie-Grace remembered how angry the director had looked the last time she'd seen him. She nodded. "I will."

The Royal Music Hall was bustling with people. Several women in matching costumes rushed down the hall, their petticoats rustling. Miss Bell's maid, Greta, passed by, too. The maid was grumbling to herself, and wisps of hair had escaped from her tight bun.

When Marie-Grace reached the second floor, she heard singing coming from her aunt's studio. The door was ajar, and she slipped inside quietly. Then she listened in wonder as Aunt Océane and Miss Bell practiced together.

Aunt Océane's voice was always beautiful, but today it sounded brighter and clearer than ever. Miss Bell had a powerful voice that soared when she hit her high notes. The prima donna was wearing a silver crown adorned with glittering stones, and the light seemed to sparkle around her.

When the song ended, Marie-Grace felt as if she had just awakened from a dream. She clapped so hard that her hands ached.

Miss Bell bowed her head, as if the applause had been only for her. Then she turned to

Aunt Océane. "We've made a good start," she said, carefully taking off her crown.

Marie-Grace could see the crown clearly now. It was a perfect circle of silver, about as tall as the palm of her hand. The entire crown was covered with jewels that flashed and shone in the light. Marie-Grace's curiosity overcame her shyness. "Are those real diamonds?" she asked.

"No, the jewels aren't real, but the crown is very valuable to me," said Miss Bell.

She explained that *The Crown Diamonds* was about a queen whose magnificent crown jewels are believed to be stolen. "I had this crown made specially for me the first time I played Queen Catarina," said Miss Bell, touching it fondly. "It brings me good luck. I wouldn't dream of playing the queen without it."

As the prima donna was talking, a towering man with reddish-brown hair and a thick beard strode into the studio. In a booming voice that matched his size, he asked Miss Bell to join him in the theater for the staging of Act One. "We won't sing, though, Sylvia," he added quickly.

"You must save your beautiful voice for the performance."

"You're so thoughtful, Roberto," said Miss Bell, gazing up at him.

Marie-Grace realized that the big, bearded man must be Roberto DiCarlo, the leading man of the opera. Although his name sounded Italian, Mr. DiCarlo spoke with an English accent. Aunt Océane greeted him politely, but he didn't answer. It was as if he hadn't even noticed that anyone but Miss Bell was in the room.

Miss Bell gathered up her shawl, and then she handed the crown to Aunt Océane. "Would you keep my crown here, Océane?" she asked. "I don't want it to get lost backstage."

Aunt Océane promised that she would keep the crown safe. She opened the antique wooden wardrobe that stood against one wall and carefully placed the crown on the top shelf.

After the two stars left together, Marie-Grace asked where Mr. DiCarlo was from. "He's English," said Aunt Océane. "His real name is Robert Charles, but he calls himself Roberto

DiCarlo because Italian opera singers are so popular." She paused. "Would you like to know a secret?"

Marie-Grace nodded eagerly.

"Well," said Aunt Océane, her voice lowered to a conspiratorial whisper. "Everyone says that Mr. DiCarlo is in love with Miss Bell. I wouldn't be surprised if they announce their engagement soon."

The handsome star is in love with the queen! Marie-Grace thought. It was like a fairy tale.

Aunt Océane showed Marie-Grace the sleeping nook she'd arranged for her. Another folding screen had been set up in the corner of the studio, and behind it there was now a cot with neatly folded blankets and an embroidered pillow. A cream-colored card rested on the pillow. Picking it up, Marie-Grace saw that Aunt Océane had drawn a pretty border of musical notes around the card. In the middle, she'd written "Welcome, Marie-Grace!"

"Thank you," she said, warmed by her aunt's kindness. She tucked the card under her pillow.

"I'm sorry that I missed our afternoon together yesterday, but I'm very glad that you will be staying here with me," said Aunt Océane. "We will have much work to do, but you will enjoy seeing the rehearsals, *non*?"

"Yes indeed!" Marie-Grace agreed.

While Aunt Océane practiced her songs at the grand piano, Marie-Grace unpacked her satchel. She hung her best dress on a peg and took out the silver-framed portrait of her mother that she always carried with her. She remembered how much her mother had loved music, and she thought Mama would have been happy to know that her daughter would someday help with an opera.

"You would have liked Aunt Océane, too, Mama," she whispered as she set the picture by the cot.

As Marie-Grace joined her aunt by the piano, Cécile arrived in a flurry of excitement. "Oh, Madame, I saw the rehearsal downstairs. The opera is going to be *fantastique*!" she exclaimed, quickly taking off her gloves.

"What can I do to help you get ready?"

Aunt Océane gave both girls sheet music and asked them to follow along as she practiced. "Please tell me if I miss anything," she said, her blue eyes worried. "I want so much to do well!"

She had just finished a song when Ida Richards, a slender young woman with light brown skin, came into the studio. Ida had a slight limp, but she held her head high as she walked.

"Ida, how nice to see you!" Aunt Océane said, putting down her music.

"Wait till you see the dress I have for you, Océane," said Ida, lifting up the large basket she was carrying. Smiling, she greeted Marie-Grace and Cécile, too.

Ida was a free woman of color, and she often made costumes for the leading performers at the Royal Music Hall. She was becoming known as one of the finest seamstresses in all of New Orleans. Marie-Grace had heard girls say that their mothers went to the opera just so that they could see Ida's new dress designs and try to copy them at home.

"I found a fabric that's just right for you," Ida told Aunt Océane. Setting down her basket, she took out a dress made of shimmering blue satin. "Come look!"

They all gathered around as Ida fluffed out the dress's fashionably full skirt. Marie-Grace ran her hand over the smooth satin. It was the deepest, richest blue that she had ever seen. Ida explained that the satin had been dyed several times just to create the special shade.

Aunt Océane went behind the screen to try on the dress. "Ida, it's lovely!" she called.

"The back still needs to be pinned. Here, let me fix it for you," said Ida. She joined Aunt Océane behind the screen.

A few moments later, Aunt Océane stepped out wearing the elegant costume. The blue satin matched her eyes and set off her fair complexion perfectly.

"Oh, it's beautiful!" said Marie-Grace.

"*Mais oui!* You look just like a queen!" Cécile declared.

"All you need is the diamond crown," added Marie-Grace.

Cécile turned to her, her eyes bright with curiosity. "A diamond crown?"

Marie-Grace asked if she could show Cécile the crown. After a moment's hesitation, Aunt Océane said, "I suppose it wouldn't hurt to look at it for a moment." Her satin dress rustling, Aunt Océane opened the door to the wardrobe, took out the crown, and handed it to Cécile.

Ida put down her pincushion and leaned forward. She drew in her breath. "My goodness! It's very pretty!"

"May I try it on?" Cécile asked.

Aunt Océane nodded, and Cécile set the sparkling crown on her head. "I feel like a princess!" she said, twirling in front of the mirror.

Next it was Marie-Grace's turn. The crown felt surprisingly heavy on her head. She gazed into the mirror and saw the diamonds flashing in the light. *They seem so real!* she thought.

She gave the crown to her aunt. "See how it looks on you," she urged Aunt Océane.

"Yes, you must!" Cécile said.

"Very well," agreed Aunt Océane, and she tried on the crown in front of the mirror.

Marie-Grace gasped when she saw her aunt's reflection. In the diamond crown and elegant satin dress, Aunt Océane really did look like a queen.

"*You* should play the queen in the opera, Aunt Océane!" exclaimed Marie-Grace.

Just then, Miss Bell entered the studio, accompanied by Greta. Miss Bell stared at Aunt Océane. Greta pursed her lips as if she'd eaten a lime.

They must have heard what I said! Marie-Grace realized. Her face turned hot with embarrassment.

Mr. Foxcroft and Mr. DiCarlo came into the room, too, along with a man of medium height with a high forehead and thinning brown hair. Mr. Foxcroft was saying, "Don't be ridiculous, Thomas."

Marie-Grace guessed that the man was Thomas Taylor, whose name she'd seen on the dressing room door. "P-Perhaps we should ask Miss Bell what she thinks," said Mr. Taylor, blinking.

Miss Bell, however, wasn't paying attention. She was still looking at Aunt Océane, who had taken off the diamond crown and was now holding it in her hands.

"I see that you were trying on my crown, Océane," Miss Bell said at last. The prima donna gave a slight laugh. But she didn't seem amused at all.

Greta turned to Miss Bell. "Should I lock the crown away in Mr. Foxcroft's office, ma'am?"

"No, I'm sure Madame Océane will take good care of it here. Won't you, Océane?" said Miss Bell. Her voice sounded unnecessarily loud. Marie-Grace saw her aunt blush.

"Of course. I'll put it away now," said Aunt Océane. She hastily put the crown back inside the wardrobe.

I never should have asked Aunt Océane to put on the crown, Marie-Grace thought. *Now she's in trouble with the prima donna—and it's my fault!*

"Océane, come downstairs with us," ordered Mr. Foxcroft. "We must work out the staging for Act Two." The director pointed to Ida. "And *you* must help us design new costumes for the chorus. The ones we brought from England were ruined during the voyage, and those other seamstresses have no imagination!"

Mr. Foxcroft suddenly caught sight of Marie-Grace and Cécile. His brows drew together in a frown, and he fixed his dark eyes on them. "You're the two girls who were spying from backstage!" he said accusingly. "What are you doing here?"

"They're helping me," said Aunt Océane. She introduced Marie-Grace and Cécile to Mr. Foxcroft, Mr. DiCarlo, and Mr. Thomas. Mr. DiCarlo was saying something to Miss Bell and didn't even acknowledge the girls. Mr. Taylor bowed politely. But Mr. Foxcroft still glared at them.

For a moment, Marie-Grace feared that the director would send them away. Then he said with a shrug, "I suppose we need as much help as we can get. But next time, don't run around like a pair of scared rabbits. If you're going to be backstage, you must make yourselves useful, do you understand?"

Both girls nodded. Mr. Foxcroft, however, had already turned to the others. "Come along now! We're wasting time and money."

"I must put a few more pins in Madame Océane's costume," said Ida.

"We'll hurry," Aunt Océane assured the director.

"I need you onstage in fifteen minutes," Mr. Foxcroft barked. "Don't be late." He strode out of the studio, accompanied by Mr. Taylor.

Miss Bell looked at Ida. "That's a lovely dress you've created for Madame Océane. I expect my new costume will be ready soon, too?"

It was more of a command than a question. Ida said that the costume would be ready very soon. "It's a beautiful silver satin, Miss Bell," she added calmly. "It will set off your crown perfectly."

"Good," said the prima donna with a curt

nod. She took Mr. DiCarlo's arm, and they left together. Greta, still scowling, followed them.

Ida rushed to finish pinning the dress. Then Aunt Océane quickly changed back into her own clothes and handed the blue dress to Marie-Grace. "Would you take this up to the sewing room?"

"I'd be happy to," said Marie-Grace. She remembered the awkward scene with Miss Bell, and she blushed again. "I'm sorry I said that you should be the queen. I think Miss Bell heard me."

"Don't worry," said Aunt Océane. She touched Marie-Grace's arm gently. "I'm sure Miss Bell knows that I'd never try to take her place."

Aunt Océane and Ida were hurrying toward the door when Aunt Océane suddenly stopped and turned back to the wardrobe. Standing on tiptoe, she reached to the top of the antique wardrobe, where a tall wooden scroll decorated the front. She fumbled for a moment behind the scroll, and then she found a key.

"I don't usually lock the wardrobe, but I will today," she said. After turning the key in the lock, Aunt Océane tucked the key back out of sight behind the wooden scroll. Then she and Ida hurried out the door.

3

A GHOST FROM THE PAST

As soon as the door shut behind Aunt Océane, Cécile crossed her arms over her chest. "Mr. Foxcroft acts as if he's king! And how dare he call us scared rabbits! I'm not scared of him— even though he looks as crafty as a fox."

"You're right!" said Marie-Grace. She giggled as she realized that Mr. Foxcroft, with his lean face and sharp dark eyes, really did look like a fox. "And Mr. DiCarlo is as big as a bear, and he's as hairy as one, too." She thought for a moment. "What about Mr. Taylor?"

"He's like *une tortue*—a turtle!" Cécile declared. Jutting her head forward, she imitated a turtle peering out from its shell and blinking its eyes.

Both girls laughed, and then Marie-Grace

picked up her aunt's costume, taking care not to get pricked by the pins. "We'd better take this upstairs."

The girls went down the hallway, and Marie-Grace opened the door to the narrow stairs that led to the third floor. The stairway was dark, and the door at the top creaked when Cécile pushed it open. They entered a long, musty-smelling hall lined with closed doors on both sides.

"Which way do we go?" Cécile asked in a low voice.

Marie-Grace looked around uncertainly. She'd been to the sewing room only once before, and Aunt Océane had led the way then. "I don't know."

Cécile put a hand on her arm. "Do you hear that noise?"

Marie-Grace listened. She could hear floorboards creaking under her feet and the tapping of rain on the roof. Then she heard another noise. It sounded like someone crying.

She gathered her courage and knocked on the

nearest door. No one answered, so she turned the knob. It was only a closet filled with boxes.

Suddenly, a door ahead flew open. A thin girl wearing an apron hurried out into the hall. She stopped short when she saw Marie-Grace and Cécile.

The girl took a step back and stared at them. "Wh-Who are you?" She had an English accent, and her eyes were swollen, as if she had been crying.

Cécile smiled at her comfortingly. "I'm Cécile, and this is Marie-Grace. What's your name?"

The girl pushed back her light brown hair. "I'm Janie." She glanced from Cécile to Marie-Grace and then back to Cécile. She looked confused. "Do you work here?"

"No, we take music lessons," Cécile said.

"Madame Océane is our teacher—and she's my aunt, too. We're helping her get ready to perform in the opera," added Marie-Grace. She gestured to the dress in her arms. "We have to take this to the sewing room. Do you know where it is?"

"There." The girl pointed down the hall. She was not much taller than Marie-Grace and Cécile, and she looked only slightly older. "Just past Greta's and my room."

"Are you with the opera company?" asked Cécile.

Janie nodded. "Miss Bell's maid, Greta, is my cousin. Greta asked if I'd come on this tour to help her, and I said yes. I thought it'd be a fine adventure to see America." She hugged her arms around herself. "Now I wish I'd never left London!"

Cécile's eyebrows shot up in surprise. "Why?"

"The voyage was terrible—worse than anything I could've imagined," said Janie. "First Miss Henrietta got sick, and we had to leave her in Cuba. Then lots of other people got sick, too. Mr. DiCarlo was so ill, he wouldn't leave his stateroom for a week. And it rained so much that water got into the trunks and ruined lots of the costumes."

Janie sniffed and then wiped her face with

her sleeve. "Maybe the ghost was haunting us even then!"

"What ghost?" Cécile and Marie-Grace asked together.

Janie stared at them. "Don't you know what happened the last time *The Crown Diamonds* was supposed to be played here?"

"Miss Bell said that something went wrong," Cécile recalled.

Marie-Grace also remembered the comment she'd overheard in the greenroom. "Do you know what happened?" she asked Janie.

"Greta told me all about it." Janie stepped closer and lowered her voice. "She heard Miss Bell talking with Mr. DiCarlo. They said that an opera company was going to perform *The Crown Diamonds* here ten years ago, but their prima donna died before opening night. She was buried in the churchyard right across the street."

"How sad!" Cécile exclaimed.

"Yes," Janie said. "And *The Crown Diamonds* hasn't been performed at the Royal Music Hall since then! A few years ago, an opera company from Paris was going to perform it here. But something even worse happened to them."

"What?" asked Marie-Grace, dreading the answer.

"When they were crossing the Atlantic, their ship went down in a terrible storm." Janie shook her head, and the shadows on the wall seemed to quiver. "They never arrived at all!"

Marie-Grace heard a scrabbling sound some-where close by, and a tingle of fear slid up her back. *It's probably just mice,* she told herself, but she edged closer to Cécile. "I've never heard anyone say that there's a ghost in the music hall," she said, trying to be brave.

"Of course people *here* wouldn't talk about it," said Janie, as if stating the obvious. "No other singers would come here if they knew about the ghost, would they?" She shuddered. "I wish I didn't have to sleep up here. I get scared at night. But Mr. Foxcroft says there's no room at the hotel for Greta and me."

Janie glanced around nervously. Then she whispered, "On our first night here, Greta looked out the window and saw the ghost coming out of the cemetery. There was hardly any light from the moon, so it was hard to see, but the ghost looked like a woman."

"Are you sure it was a ghost?" asked Cécile in a hushed voice.

Janie nodded. "Greta didn't know what it was at first, but then she heard about the singer who died, and it all made sense. Don't you see what's happening?" Janie asked, her eyes red-rimmed against her pale skin. "The ghost doesn't want anyone to put on *The Crown Diamonds* here, and it's coming to haunt us!"

Without another word, Janie slipped past the girls and rushed down the stairs.

After Janie left, the hall seemed gloomier than ever. *Could there really be a ghost here?* Marie-Grace worried as she and Cécile headed down the hall. They found the sewing room and left Aunt Océane's costume there. Then

Marie-Grace glanced out the sewing room's window. "You *can* see the cemetery," she told Cécile.

Both girls peered out the window. It was cloudy outside, and a gaslight was shining by the gate to the cemetery. Marie-Grace shivered and turned away.

She and Cécile hurried downstairs to Aunt Océane's studio. Cécile's maid was waiting there for them. "Thank heavens you've returned, Miss Cécile!" the young maid greeted them. "I was scared waiting for you here by myself, with those noises."

Marie-Grace and Cécile shared a glance. Then Cécile asked, "What noises?"

The maid looked around anxiously. "It was like scratching in the walls. I heard it only a moment ago."

They all listened, but the room was silent. "It was there before, I promise you," the maid told the girls. She gathered up Cécile's gloves and cloak. "We must go now, Miss Cécile, or your mother will be worried."

Marie-Grace felt a chill. *Was it only mice that the maid had heard?* she wondered.

"I'll be back on Tuesday, if I can," Cécile told Marie-Grace. Then she added in a lower voice, "Be careful."

4
An Intruder

That night, Marie-Grace went to bed while her aunt was still rehearsing downstairs. As she drifted off to sleep, she listened for sounds in the walls. All she heard was the creaking of the old building.

An hour or so later, she woke up with a start. For a moment, she forgot where she was. Then she heard Aunt Océane talking quietly on the other side of the screen. "I understand why you need to leave, Ida. But I shall miss you. You've been such a good friend to me."

"I'll miss you, too," said Ida. "You're the only person here I could have trusted with my secret. And don't worry, I'll finish your costume before I leave. It will be beautiful!"

Ida's leaving? Why? wondered Marie-Grace.

And why is it a secret? But she was tired, and she was glad that Aunt Océane was close by. She nestled her head back on the pillow.

Poor Janie! she thought as she fell asleep again. *I'd hate to be sleeping on the top floor with only sour-faced Greta for company.*

Marie-Grace slept late the next morning. By the time she'd dressed and eaten a croissant for breakfast, rehearsals had begun. She saw Louis in the hall downstairs, and he told her that a messenger had delivered a note for her.

Marie-Grace knew that the note must be from Papa. Ever since the terrible yellow fever epidemic last summer, her father had tried never to be away from home overnight. When he had to take care of patients at night, he always sent a message telling Marie-Grace and their house-keeper where he was and when he'd return. Today he'd written:

My dear daughter,

I am still aboard the ship Georgia.
*We've had a few more cases of this puzzling
fever, and other ships have reported it, too.
Fortunately, no one has died, although many
of my patients are still quite ill. Some have
sore throats, and others have pain and ringing
in their ears. I will likely be here for another
day or more.*

*I hope you and your Aunt Océane are
well. If you need me, send a message to
the* Georgia.

Papa

Marie-Grace tucked the note into her pocket.
Then she went backstage. She found her aunt in
her dressing room, a small room next to Miss
Bell's larger dressing room. Aunt Océane was
trying to learn the words to a duet she would be
singing with Mr. DiCarlo.

"Mr. DiCarlo already knows the song, and
he doesn't want to practice it with me," said
Aunt Océane. She handed Marie-Grace sheets

of music. "Will you take his part so that I can practice mine?"

Marie-Grace was glad to help. In the deepest voice she could manage, she was singing, "If I could but courage feel…" when there was a knock at the door, and Greta called Aunt Océane back to the stage.

Marie-Grace asked what she should do during the rehearsal. Aunt Océane suggested that she help Bridget and Sophie, the two seamstresses who were making costumes for the chorus. Marie-Grace found the seamstresses in the greenroom, measuring out material. Sophie, a small blonde woman, asked Marie-Grace if she would sew the hems of some skirts.

"Yes," said Marie-Grace. She wasn't an expert seamstress, but she knew how to hem a skirt. "I can do that."

Bridget, a dark-haired young woman with a smattering of freckles, handed Marie-Grace a white skirt that had already been pinned, along with a pincushion, a needle, and thread. "As soon as you've finished, I'll have another one for you," said Bridget, looking at the pile of costumes in front of her.

The greenroom was crowded with people and costumes, so Marie-Grace took the skirt into her aunt's dressing room. Sitting at the dressing table, she made careful stitches in the skirt's stiff white fabric. *When I see the chorus onstage, I'll know that I helped make their costumes,* she thought, smiling to herself.

As she stitched, Marie-Grace heard lovely singing from the rehearsal. But there was also shouting from Mr. Foxcroft. "No, no, no! How many times do I have to tell you that's wrong?" she heard him bellow at the chorus. "You must do it again."

Marie-Grace was halfway through a stitch when the door of a dressing room banged nearby. Then she heard a furious, high-pitched yowl.

Her heart pounding, Marie-Grace sat up straight, listening hard. For a moment she wondered if the sound had come from the stage, but it had seemed closer than that. She looked into the hall. The doors to the dressing rooms on either side of her were shut. People were gathered in the greenroom, talking loudly. Nothing seemed out of the ordinary. Marie-Grace closed the door and went back to her sewing.

She had just bent over her stitching again when a bloodcurdling scream split the air. Then a door slammed. Marie-Grace threw down her sewing and ran out into the hall. She found Greta pointing to the closed door of Miss Bell's dressing room.

"Heaven help us," the maid cried as members of the opera company came running. "There's a cat in Miss Bell's dressing room!"

That's what I heard, Marie-Grace realized. She didn't understand why Greta seemed so afraid. *It's just a cat,* she thought. But when Aunt Océane and the other performers arrived a moment later, they looked worried, too.

"Get it out of my dressing room this instant!" the prima donna exclaimed. She held a lacy handkerchief to her nose as another yowl rose from behind her dressing room door.

Looks of concern flashed among the members

of the company. Janie, who was standing close to Marie-Grace, groaned, "Oh no!"

Mr. Foxcroft hurried down the hall. "What's this I hear about a cat?"

"A cat has appeared in Sylvia's dressing room," Mr. DiCarlo announced in his booming voice. "She's upset, of course." He put his arm around Miss Bell protectively.

"I'll take care of it," said Mr. Foxcroft. The music director flung open the door, and Marie-Grace glimpsed a skinny black cat with a patch of white on its tail. The cat was standing in the far corner with its back arched. Mr. Foxcroft marched in as if he were going to battle and slammed the door behind himself. The members of the company stood in the hall, talking in hushed tones.

"Why is everyone so upset?" Marie-Grace whispered to Janie. "I've heard performers say that cats are good luck."

"Miss Bell can't abide cats," Janie whispered back. "When she's around them, she sneezes and she can hardly breathe." Janie's voice dropped even lower. "She once walked out of a performance because a cat was backstage."

Mr. Foxcroft emerged from the dressing room. Sweat dripped down his face, and his cheeks were flushed. "That cat is vicious!" he muttered. He dusted off his white-gloved hands. "I couldn't even get near it."

Marie-Grace felt sorry for the trapped cat. Suddenly she thought of someone who liked animals. "I'll ask Louis to help," she offered.

She found Louis by the back door. When she told him what the problem was, he went into a closet and brought out a large wicker basket. He put a piece of meat from his lunch into the basket. Then he and Marie-Grace walked quickly to Miss Bell's dressing room. As the cast members watched from a safe distance, Louis carried the basket inside.

A few minutes later, Louis came out. He'd taken off his jacket, and it was now stretched tightly across the top of the basket. Howls of protest and scratching noises could be heard from inside the basket. As he passed by, Louis told Marie-Grace, "I know this cat—he lives in the alley. I'll put him back outside."

Many of the cast members applauded as Louis carried the basket away. But Marie-Grace saw Mr. DiCarlo frown. "Something strange is going on here," he complained, his loud voice filling the hallway. "Why did a cat go into Miss Bell's dressing room, of all places?"

Why indeed? Marie-Grace wondered. *And how did it get there?* She was sure that all the dressing room doors had been closed.

She heard the people around her talking, everyone wondering aloud what could have happened.

"Maybe it was the ghost!" Greta blurted out. All the cast members looked at her. From their expressions, Marie-Grace guessed that the whole cast had heard about the singer who had died at the Royal Music Hall.

Miss Bell held Mr. DiCarlo's arm for support. "Perhaps it's a sign," she said nervously. "Maybe we shouldn't perform *The Crown Diamonds* here. We could choose another opera."

"Or we could pack up and go on to St. Louis," Mr. DiCarlo suggested. He gazed down at Miss Bell fondly. "Sylvia and I could begin our tour there instead."

"That's an excellent idea!" agreed Miss Bell, nodding so hard that her blonde ringlets bounced.

Marie-Grace's heart sank. If the company changed its plans now, Aunt Océane would never get to sing her role.

Mr. Foxcroft's dark eyes scanned the assembled cast. "I won't have any more foolish talk about a ghost!" he declared. "Advertisements for *The Crown Diamonds* are in the newspapers, and ticket sales are going well. I didn't know about the so-called ghost when I planned this tour, and it's too late to change now. We must go ahead with the opera."

He raised his voice. "Back to work, everyone. We'll start with Act Three now. We'll run straight through to the final scene, where the queen wears her crown."

Aunt Océane beckoned to Marie-Grace.

"Would you get the crown, please?" she asked. "It's in the wardrobe."

Marie-Grace nodded and hurried up to the second floor. Inside her aunt's studio, she stood on a footstool and reached up to the top of the wardrobe. She felt around behind the wooden scroll until her fingers found the cold metal key. Then she unlocked the wardrobe.

Moving the footstool aside, she opened the door and reached for the crown on the top shelf. Her hands felt only empty space where the crown had been.

That's strange, she thought.

She grabbed the footstool again. Standing on it, she carefully looked inside the wardrobe. There were only folded clothes on the top shelf.

Her heart beating fast, Marie-Grace searched the other shelves, too. She hoped that the crown might be hidden behind something, so she pushed aside all the clothes and reached into the farthest corners. There was nothing.

The diamond crown was gone.

5
SEARCH FOR A CROWN

Marie-Grace flew down the stairs, almost tripping on the next-to-last step. She ran all the way to the backstage, where Aunt Océane was standing in the wings. "I can't find the crown," she told her aunt breathlessly. "It's not in the wardrobe."

Aunt Océane's eyes widened. "It must be there. Perhaps you missed it. I'll look." She gathered up her skirts and rushed upstairs, with Marie-Grace close behind her.

Together, they searched the wardrobe again. "It's gone," Aunt Océane admitted at last. She turned to Marie-Grace. "Is it possible that you or Cécile took out the crown after I left?"

"No," said Marie-Grace, looking up at her

aunt. "I promise you, we never would have taken it."

"Of course you wouldn't have," said Aunt Océane. She sighed and shut the wardrobe door. "I just can't think how it vanished. But I must go and tell the others."

Marie-Grace dreaded facing Miss Bell and Mr. Foxcroft with the bad news. The director's reaction was even worse than she had feared.

"GONE!" he thundered as the singers gathered onstage. "What do you mean, it's gone?"

Aunt Océane explained what had happened.

"I've never performed *The Crown Diamonds* without my crown!" Miss Bell protested.

Queen Catarina's throne had been set in the middle of the stage, and now Miss Bell slumped down into it. "First everyone on the ship becomes sick, then a black cat appears in my dressing room, and now my diamond crown has disappeared. Perhaps the ghost really is haunting me!" She buried her head in her hands.

Mr. Foxcroft turned to Aunt Océane. "The crown was left with you. How could it be lost?"

Aunt Océane flushed. "I don't know! I locked the wardrobe before I left the room. It was still locked when Marie-Grace went to get the crown just now."

Mr. Foxcroft glared at Marie-Grace. "What about you? You were in that room alone. Did you take the crown while everyone else was gone?"

The cast turned toward her, and Marie-Grace felt them staring. She wanted to say that she'd never do such a thing. But her mouth was dry, and words seemed to desert her.

Then she felt her aunt's comforting arm around her shoulders. "Marie-Grace would never steal anything," said Aunt Océane in her strong voice. "I would trust her with my life. Indeed, she once helped save my life."

Her aunt's kind words echoed in Marie-Grace's heart. She stood tall as the director began to pace across the stage.

For a few moments, the only sounds were the taps of Mr. Foxcroft's polished black boots on the wooden stage. Then the director whirled around to face the assembly. "Well, *someone* took the crown," he declared. "Does anyone know who it could have been?"

Marie-Grace heard a whisper behind her. "This is all Océane's fault. *She* was supposed to watch over the crown."

Suddenly, Mr. Taylor spoke up. "No one should worry about ghosts," he said with a glance toward Miss Bell. "Perhaps a thief broke in and stole the crown in order to sell it," Mr. Taylor suggested. He blinked nervously. "Someone from outside the opera company might not have known that the diamonds were fake."

Some people agreed that this might be possible. But Marie-Grace wondered, *How could a thief from outside have known that the crown was in Aunt Océane's wardrobe?*

One woman suggested that the police should be called in. Mr. Foxcroft brushed that idea aside. "The last thing we need is for the police to be involved. We want only *good* publicity."

"But if we don't catch the thief, I'll never get my crown back!" Miss Bell wailed. "And I can't perform *The Crown Diamonds* without it."

Mr. DiCarlo turned to the director. "If Miss Bell doesn't have her crown, she won't go onstage—and I won't either."

The stage went silent. If both stars refused to perform, the show might be canceled.

Mr. Foxcroft pressed his hands to his temples as if his head hurt. Marie-Grace waited anxiously for his reply. Finally the director said quietly, "This is our first performance in America, and it may determine our future here," he reminded the cast. "If we are successful in New Orleans, we will be reviewed in all the newspapers. People everywhere will read about us." Mr. Foxcroft turned to the two stars and smiled craftily. "You *do* want it to be a success, don't you?"

"Oh yes, of course!" said Miss Bell. "Our American debut means a great deal to both Roberto and me." She looked up at Mr. DiCarlo, and the leading man nodded.

Thank heavens! thought Marie-Grace.

"Well then, why don't we get back to work?" the director said. "After all, the crown might simply have been misplaced somehow—these things happen all the time, you know. Perhaps Océane only thought she locked the wardrobe. Perhaps someone picked up the crown and then set it with other costumes by mistake." He turned to Miss Bell's maid. "Greta, go look through all the costumes. Get Janie to help you. Search everywhere you can think of," he added. Then he waved a hand at the cast and ordered, "Everyone else, get back to rehearsal."

Greta headed backstage with Janie. Marie-Grace decided to follow them. "I can't imagine that crown would just be lying about," Greta grumbled. "But I suppose we must look anyway."

As they entered the cluttered greenroom, Marie-Grace saw costumes piled everywhere. I'll start here," said Greta with a sigh. "Janie, you look through the dressing rooms."

"I can help," Marie-Grace offered.

Greta narrowed her eyes, as if suspicious of any help Marie-Grace might offer. But Janie piped up eagerly. "Oh yes, it'll go faster if there are two of us."

"Very well," said Greta. "You girls stay together, though. And tell me at once if you find the crown."

Marie-Grace and Janie started on the dressing rooms. Although the actors had been in the theater for only a few days, their dressing rooms already reflected their personalities. Aunt Océane's small space was clean and tidy, and it smelled of the light, lavender-scented perfume she always wore. Two costumes hung from pegs on the wall, and Marie-Grace's sewing supplies were in a basket by the table. Otherwise the room was empty.

Miss Bell's dressing room smelled of heavy perfume. Her dressing table was filled with jars of skin creams and face powders, all carefully arranged. Even her earrings were lined up in glittering rows. Several costumes had been neatly hung on pegs.

"If anyone had put the crown in here, Greta would've seen it already," said Janie after they looked through the costumes, and Marie-Grace agreed.

The doors to Mr. DiCarlo's and Mr. Taylor's dressing rooms were open, so the girls checked there next.

Mr. DiCarlo's room smelled of pipe smoke, and his dressing table was littered with bottles of hair ointments and medicines. Music magazines were strewn around the room. Marie-Grace saw articles about composers such as Mozart and Beethoven and reviews of operas from around the world. The pegs on the walls were crowded with costumes, and more costumes were heaped on the floor. Together, Marie-Grace and Janie looked through them all, but the crown wasn't there.

Mr. Taylor's dressing room was the plainest of the stars' rooms. The dressing table held only a hairbrush and some yellowed reviews of past operas that he had performed in. Marie-Grace noticed that Mr. Taylor had never been the leading man, but he had sung in many cities. A single well-worn suit jacket hung from a peg on the wall. The room seemed forlorn after Mr. DiCarlo's crowded dressing room.

Poor Mr. Taylor, thought Marie-Grace as they left his dressing room. *It must be hard to be a turtle next to a bear.*

At the end of the hall, a door boasted a freshly painted sign with elegant gold lettering. It read:

Mr. Charles Foxcroft
Owner and Director
Foxcroft's World-Famous London Opera Company

The door was open slightly, and Marie-Grace peeked inside. Mr. Foxcroft had taken as his personal office a long room that looked as if it had once been a dressing room for half a dozen people. There were two big windows, and mirrors along the wall reflected light throughout the room. A large mahogany table stacked high with books, musical scores, and papers took up the center of the room. Costumes were draped over the chairs, and an open crate filled with costumes sat nearby, brightly colored dresses spilling out of it.

Marie-Grace had just taken the first costume
out of the crate when Greta's sharp voice inter-
rupted her. "I asked you girls to look in the
dressing rooms, not Mr. Foxcroft's office! I'll go
through this room myself."

Janie jumped nervously. "But Greta, we've
already looked in the dressing rooms," she
explained.

"Then go upstairs to Madame Océane's
studio," Greta told her impatiently. "If the crown
is anywhere, that's the most likely place. And
check the sewing room, too. The seamstresses
might have picked it up with other costumes."
With a wave of her hand, Greta shooed the girls
out the door.

In the hallway, they saw Miss Bell. Her
cheeks were pink, and she seemed flustered.
"Where's Greta?" she demanded.

Janie gestured toward the office. "In there,
ma'am."

"Greta!" the prima donna trilled, opening the
door to the office. "Greta, I need your help now!"

Marie-Grace and Janie went up to Aunt

Océane's studio. When they reached it, Marie-Grace discovered that her aunt was already there.

"I've been looking through the whole room," said Aunt Océane, her forehead creased with worry. The girls helped her search. They checked beneath the pillows, under the chairs and sofa, beside the piano, and behind the curtains. The crown was nowhere to be found.

Finally, Aunt Océane returned to the theater, and Marie-Grace and Janie climbed the narrow stairs to the third floor. The dim hall was silent, and every door was closed. Marie-Grace knocked on the sewing room door.

When Ida opened it, she seemed tense. "Yes?" she asked.

Through the open door, Marie-Grace could see costumes scattered on the worktable. She explained that she and Janie were searching for the crown. "Mr. Foxcroft says it might have been picked up with some costumes. Could we look?"

To Marie-Grace's surprise, Ida shook her

head no. "Bridget and Sophie told me about the missing crown," she said abruptly. "We went through the costumes, and it's not here. I must get on with my sewing now. Why don't you girls look somewhere else?"

Ida shut the door, leaving the girls in the hallway. Marie-Grace had a hollow feeling in her stomach as she stared at the closed door. *Ida was so friendly before. What's wrong now?*

The girls checked the other doors along the hall. Most were locked. Some opened onto storage rooms where the dust was so thick, it was obvious that nothing had been disturbed in a long time.

"This is where Greta and I sleep," said Janie as she opened the last door. The small room was lit by a single large window. The only furnishings were two cots, an old wardrobe, and a worn chair. It didn't take the girls long to search through everything. There were lots of cobwebs, but no crown.

"I never thought the crown was simply lost," said Janie when they finally gave up. She stood by the window. "I think the ghost took it."

The cold room suddenly seemed to get even chillier. Marie-Grace joined Janie by the window. Leaning on the windowsill, she could see the cemetery across the street. Late-afternoon shadows stretched across the graves, darkening the tombstones. "There's no such thing as ghosts," she said, hoping it was true.

"No, you're wrong!" Janie shook her head, her wispy brown hair flying. "Remember I told you that Greta *saw* it coming from the cemetery the first night we were here?" Janie's eyes were wide with fear.

"Yes, I remember," said Marie-Grace slowly.

"Well, last night I couldn't sleep because Greta was snoring so loud. I got up and looked out this window. *I* saw the ghost then."

"What did it look like?"

"The night was so dark, I couldn't tell. I just saw it coming straight out of the cemetery, and it was headed this way." Janie glanced out the window again, as if she half expected the ghost to reappear. "I'm scared!"

Marie-Grace wished with all her heart that Cécile were there with them. *Cécile wouldn't be scared,* she thought. But now it was up to Marie-Grace to be the brave one.

6
OVERHEARD

"Let's go downstairs," Marie-Grace told Janie, trying to sound more confident than she felt. "Greta might've found the crown by now."

Marie-Grace led the way down the narrow stairway to the second floor. The girls hurried on to the lobby.

When they reached the greenroom, however, Greta was nowhere in sight. Janie knocked on the door to Miss Bell's dressing room, but no one answered. Mr. Foxcroft's office door was ajar, and the girls looked in. Greta wasn't there.

Marie-Grace was about to leave when she noticed that the dress she had taken out of the crate earlier was still exactly where she'd left it. She crossed the office and looked into the crate. None of the other costumes had been moved, either.

"Greta hasn't searched here yet," she told Janie. "Why don't we look?" Marie-Grace began pulling costumes out of the crate.

Standing in the doorway, Janie hesitated. "Are you sure we should?"

Why can't Janie be just a little bit brave? wondered Marie-Grace. Then she remembered that Janie was in a strange city, without any family except stern Greta. *It must be hard for her,* she thought.

"Mr. Foxcroft said to look everywhere," Marie-Grace reminded her. "What if the crown is right here?"

Janie edged into the office, and the door swung nearly shut behind her. "All right," she said reluctantly. "But I hope Greta doesn't find us."

Marie-Grace set to work digging through the crate. She searched quickly, pulling out men's old-fashioned doublets and breeches and ladies' silk dresses and starched petticoats.

All of the costumes were well worn, and some had holes in them.

At last she reached the bottom of the crate. "The crown isn't in this box," she told Janie.

As she started putting the costumes back, she glanced over her shoulder. Janie was staring at the papers on the mahogany table. "There are an awful lot of bills here!" she exclaimed. "One says that Mr. Foxcroft owes hundreds of pounds in London. Can you imagine owing so much?"

Marie-Grace didn't know how much a pound was worth in dollars, but it sounded like a lot of money. "No, I can't," she said. "Maybe that's why Mr. Foxcroft is always getting angry."

Marie-Grace had just finished stuffing the costumes back into the crate when she heard the director's voice down the hall. "Greta," he was saying, "I need to talk to you. Come into my office."

"Oh no!" Janie dropped the paper she'd been holding and looked around in a panic. "We can't let them find us!" She pulled on Marie-Grace's arm. "Under here," she whispered, diving beneath the mahogany table.

Marie-Grace didn't want to hide from Greta and Mr. Foxcroft—but she didn't want Janie to get into trouble, either. After a moment's hesitation, she crouched under the table, too, crawling out of sight just as she heard the door swing open. From under the table, Marie-Grace could see Mr. Foxcroft's polished black boots and Greta's sturdy work boots.

"Have you found the crown yet, Greta?" demanded Mr. Foxcroft.

"No, sir," she replied. "I'm not expecting that I *will* find it, either."

The director sighed. "And why is that?"

"Because it's the ghost's work, that's why!" Greta said grimly. "I've *seen* the ghost, sir, and Janie has, too. I know it's real! Why else would everything be going wrong?"

Marie-Grace felt Janie tense beside her.

"Don't be foolish," Mr. Foxcroft replied sharply. "If the crown is missing, it's because a flesh-and-blood person took it—not some imaginary ghost."

Mr. Foxcroft slammed something down on the table above the girls' heads. Marie-Grace felt the table shake. She tried to tuck herself into a tight ball. *What will happen if Mr. Foxcroft sees us here?* she worried.

Greta's next words made her catch her breath.

"Well, then, Madame Océane must be to blame," the maid said angrily. "I saw how she looked at my mistress's crown. She wishes that *she* could play the queen's role. Maybe she took the crown because she wants Miss Bell to quit."

"That's possible," Mr. Foxcroft said slowly. "To be honest, I have my suspicions about Madame Océane. We don't know much about her, do we? Watch her carefully, Greta, and let me know if you discover anything. But, whatever you do, don't mention the ghost again. I have enough trouble as it is."

Marie-Grace heard the shuffle of footsteps and the sound of the door closing. The voices faded away. Marie-Grace and Janie waited a few moments. Then they crawled from their hiding place and slipped out of the office.

Marie-Grace's face burned with anger. *How dare they say such terrible things about Aunt Océane!* she thought.

She turned to Janie. "You don't believe what they said about my aunt, do you?"

"No," said Janie. "I'm sure your aunt didn't steal the crown. I *know* it was the ghost." She glanced down the hall of dressing rooms. "And I'm afraid something even worse is going to happen next."

That night while Aunt Océane was rehearsing, Marie-Grace tossed and turned on the narrow cot in the studio. She finally fell asleep, but she woke again not much later. On the other side of the screen she saw the glow of a light, and she heard the scratching of a pen.

Marie-Grace got up and wrapped her shawl around her shoulders. She found Aunt Océane writing at her desk by the light of a candle.

"I can't sleep, so I decided to write to your

Uncle Luc," her aunt said. She rested her pen on the ink bottle. "I keep thinking about the crown. I don't understand what could have happened to it. And finding the cat in the dressing room was strange, too. It's almost as if someone *wants* the opera to fail. But that's silly, isn't it?"

Or is it? Marie-Grace wondered. She remembered what Janie had said about the shadowy figure coming from the cemetery at night, and she tugged her shawl tighter. By the flickering light of the candle, strange things seemed more possible than ever.

"Aunt Océane, do you think that a ghost could be haunting the opera?"

"Non. We have had bad luck, though, and some people want to blame it on..." Aunt Océane hesitated. "On other things." A shadow of sadness passed over her face.

She knows that people think she took the crown, Marie-Grace realized with a pang.

Aunt Océane patted her hand reassuringly. "You go to bed now. Sleep well, and don't worry."

As she returned to her bed, though, Marie-Grace couldn't help but worry. *It's not fair that Aunt Océane is being blamed!* she thought. *If only I knew who really stole the crown.*

7

JUST A SCRATCH

The next morning, while the actors gathered backstage, Marie-Grace sewed in her aunt's dressing room. She had just noticed that the theater was strangely quiet when there was a knock at the door. "Mr. Foxcroft is back, and there's a meeting onstage," one of the stage crew announced.

Marie-Grace's stomach knotted. *Where has Mr. Foxcroft been?* she wondered. *Has something else gone wrong?* When she reached the stage, she saw that the director's white hair was unkempt, and a thin, angry red line ran down his cheek.

"What happened?" asked Mr. Taylor, pointing to the red scratch.

"Oh, I cut myself while shaving," said Mr. Foxcroft as everyone gathered onstage.

A slight smile creased his lean face. "Maybe I should grow a beard like Mr. DiCarlo, eh?"

Several members of the cast laughed, but when Marie-Grace glanced over at Mr. DiCarlo, she saw that he was staring into space, as if he hadn't even heard the director. *He must be worried about Miss Bell*, she thought.

Mr. Foxcroft called for everyone's attention. "Some of you have been saying that we'll have bad luck with *The Crown Diamonds*. And perhaps there have been a few problems so far."

Someone behind Marie-Grace whispered, "He's right about that!"

"But I have good news." Mr. Foxcroft held up a black ledger book. "The theater is sold out for opening night."

Cast members clapped.

"Furthermore," said Mr. Foxcroft, "I've found a skilled craftsman who will make Miss Bell a new crown before opening night. It will look exactly like the old crown! Of course, it will be expensive to have it made so quickly. But if Miss Bell will agree to continue with the opera,

I shall gladly pay for the replacement."

Everyone turned to look at Miss Bell. The prima donna hesitated. Mr. DiCarlo leaned over and said something to her. Marie-Grace held her breath. *If only Miss Bell says yes!*

"I do hope you'll agree, Sylvia," Mr. Foxcroft added. "The people of New Orleans can hardly wait to hear you and Mr. DiCarlo sing. And newspaper reporters are planning to write special stories about your first performance in America."

Miss Bell sighed, and then she nodded as regally as if she really were a queen. "Well, in that case, I can hardly refuse, can I?"

Cheers and applause broke out among the cast members. Marie-Grace was relieved to see Aunt Océane smiling, too. As the chorus was called to rehearse, Marie-Grace went back to the dressing room with her aunt.

"Would you go to the post office next door and mail my letter to your Uncle Luc?" Aunt Océane asked.

"I'd be glad to," said Marie-Grace. She

gathered up her shawl, and her aunt gave her the letter and a coin for postage.

As she was leaving, Marie-Grace saw Louis by the back entrance. He gave her a note from Papa. Her father had written that his patients aboard the *Georgia* were getting better, and he hoped that his work there would be done soon. "I should be home in time for the opera's opening night," Papa had added.

Hurrah! thought Marie-Grace as she tucked the note away.

It was drizzling outside, and she pulled her shawl over her head. She was about to step outside when she saw a mouse dart across the narrow alleyway. Marie-Grace paused in the doorway. "Louis, why do you think that black cat was in the music hall yesterday? Could it have come inside to chase mice? I think I heard some mice in the walls."

Louis stood in the open doorway with her. "There are mice in every old building. But there are a lot more rats and mice to chase out here. So why would an alley cat want to go inside?"

He shook his head. "Non, I think someone *took* that cat inside the building."

"Are you sure the cat didn't just wander in?"

"I know that cat," Louis said firmly. "He doesn't like being near people. He never would have come inside willingly."

Marie-Grace nodded. She'd seen the cat with his back up, hissing. *If someone had tried to pick up that cat, he would have fought hard*, she thought. She hadn't noticed scratches on anyone's hands or arms, but the stars of the opera company dressed formally while working, and both men and women often wore white gloves. *If they'd been wearing gloves, though, maybe their hands wouldn't have been scratched.*

She remembered the mark on Mr. Foxcroft's face this morning. Had it been there yesterday? She didn't recall seeing it, but she knew that a scratch sometimes looked worse the day *after* it happened.

Could Mr. Foxcroft have been lying when he said he hadn't been able to get near the cat in the dressing room? Marie-Grace wondered. *Or was he the one who'd brought the cat into the dressing room in the first place?*

She couldn't think of any reason why Mr. Foxcroft would have played such a mean trick on Miss Bell. Her stomach clenched as the thought came to her, *Maybe it **is** the ghost who's causing all the trouble.*

Hesitantly, she asked Louis if he knew about the singer who had died.

Louis frowned. "Where did you hear about that?"

"Some people are saying that the singer's ghost is haunting the opera," she explained. "They say that the ghost doesn't want anyone to perform *The Crown Diamonds* here. Is that true?"

"You mustn't pay attention to talk about ghosts, Marie-Grace," said Louis. But he admitted that a tragedy had occurred ten years ago when an opera company had come to the Royal Music Hall to perform *The Crown Diamonds*. "The prima donna, a woman named Angélique..." Louis hesitated. "I can't remember her last name," he said finally. "Anyway, she became ill and died just before the show began. It was very sad." He sighed. "I remember that she had a voice like an angel's. The opera couldn't go on without her."

Janie was right, Marie-Grace realized with a shiver. *There **was** a prima donna who died!*

She swallowed hard before she asked her next question. "Is it true that another company was going to perform *The Crown Diamonds* here, but their ship was lost at sea?"

"Yes..." Louis said slowly. "But it happened in a terrible storm, and other ships were lost, too. It had nothing to do with the opera. It was just bad luck."

That's an awful lot of bad luck for one opera, thought Marie-Grace as she went down the alley and around the building to the main avenue.

Across the street, she saw the cemetery looming in the mist. The graveyard looked forlorn, and Marie-Grace was glad that the street was bustling with activity. Carriages rolled past, and people carrying umbrellas strolled along the banquette, some speaking French, others English. A dark-skinned woman with a bright kerchief on her head called out, *"Pralines! Fresh, sweet pralines!"* The rich pecan pralines smelled heavenly, and Marie-Grace wished she had enough money to buy some.

She entered the post office and took her place in line. The line moved slowly because the red-haired clerk at the window chatted with every customer. When Marie-Grace reached the window, the clerk carefully looked at Aunt Océane's letter. "This is from Madame Rousseau at the Royal Music Hall."

"Yes, sir," said Marie-Grace, giving him the coin for postage. "Madame Rousseau is my aunt."

"Ah," said the clerk, reaching into the wooden mail slots lined up like tiny horses' stalls behind the window. "Then perhaps you would like to give her this letter?" He handed her an envelope with Uncle Luc's familiar writing on the front. He smiled. *"Monsieur* Rousseau has also written to Madame Rousseau. The letter arrived today."

"Thank you," said Marie-Grace, who knew

that her aunt would be glad to get word from Uncle Luc.

When she got back to the Royal Music Hall, Marie-Grace saw that more people had gathered to buy tickets for *The Crown Diamonds*. A hand-lettered sign by the ticket window read: "Only a Few Tickets Still Available for Opening Night."

That's strange, thought Marie-Grace as she climbed the steps to the front hall. *Mr. Foxcroft said that opening night was sold out.*

Backstage, she found Aunt Océane in her dressing room. Her aunt looked tired, but her eyes brightened when Marie-Grace gave her Uncle Luc's letter. She was poring over the long letter when Greta's voice sounded through the door. "Madame Océane, you must hurry," she scolded. "Everyone is waiting for you onstage!"

"I'm so sorry!" called Aunt Océane. Quickly putting away the letter, she rushed off, closing the door behind her.

Marie-Grace picked up the costume she had been hemming earlier that morning. As she made small, careful stitches, she heard two women talking in low voices in the hallway. "Madame Océane is causing everyone trouble," said one woman. "I wouldn't be surprised if *she* took the crown—and put the cat in Miss Bell's dressing room, too."

"Do you really think so?" the other woman asked.

"Of course," said the first woman. "Who else but Madame Océane will benefit if Miss Bell quits the opera?"

"Perhaps you're right," the second woman said. "But what a terrible thing to do! If people heard about it, Madame Océane would never be hired to sing in New Orleans again. She'd have to move away."

Marie-Grace dropped her sewing. *Aunt Océane would never hurt anyone!* she wanted to shout. She rushed to the door and looked out to see who had been speaking. But the women had disappeared down the hall.

Marie-Grace shut the door again. If those two women were saying such awful things about Aunt Océane, what was everyone else saying?

Marie-Grace couldn't bear to think of Aunt Océane being treated so unfairly. She was so upset that when someone rapped at the door, she didn't even want to answer it. Then another knock sounded, louder this time.

"Who is it?" Marie-Grace called.

"Me!" Cécile burst in, her wool cloak damp with rain. "And I brought lots of treats. They're *délicieux*!" Smiling, she held up a large basket covered with a cloth. Her smile faded when she looked at Marie-Grace. "What's wrong? You look as if you've seen a ghost."

"It's even worse than that," Marie-Grace said. "Oh, Cécile, the crown has disappeared, and people are blaming Aunt Océane. We have to help her."

8
ON PINS AND NEEDLES

Marie-Grace quickly gathered up her sewing, and she and Cécile went upstairs to Aunt Océane's studio.

"So much has gone wrong," Marie-Grace began as she closed the door behind them. She set her sewing on the table. "None of it is Aunt Océane's fault, but people are blaming her anyway."

Cécile tossed her cloak over a chair and put down the basket she'd brought. Then she sat down and listened closely as Marie-Grace told her how the black cat had mysteriously appeared in Miss Bell's dressing room and the crown had disappeared from the wardrobe.

"Everyone's upset. Janie is sure that the ghost is causing all the problems." Marie-Grace lowered her voice. "Janie said she saw the ghost herself last night. It was coming from the cemetery, right toward the Royal Music Hall."

Cécile leaned forward in her chair. "Do you think that's *true*?"

"I don't know what to think," said Marie-Grace. "Louis says not to pay attention to talk of a ghost. Still, a lot of bad things have happened. It can't all be just by chance."

"The cat *could* have wandered in by itself," Cécile suggested.

"Yes, but someone *must've* taken the crown," said Marie-Grace. "You and I both saw Aunt Océane lock it in the wardrobe, and now it's gone. Mr. Taylor says a thief from outside the opera might have stolen the crown. But I heard people whispering about Aunt Océane, too."

"Whispering what? Why would they blame Madame Océane?" Cécile asked indignantly. "It wasn't her fault that the crown was taken from the wardrobe."

"Of course not!" Marie-Grace agreed warmly. "But that crown was very important to Miss Bell. She even said that she wouldn't play the role of queen without it."

"Really?"

"Yes! And Aunt Océane is Miss Bell's understudy," Marie-Grace continued. "So if Miss Bell quits the show…" Marie-Grace didn't even want to finish her sentence.

Cécile finished it for her. "Then Madame Océane would take the part, and *she* would be the star of the opera instead of Miss Bell."

Marie-Grace nodded.

Cécile's eyes widened. "Madame Océane would *never* steal anything—even if she did want to be the queen."

"I know! But people in the opera company don't know that. And their gossip could spread all over New Orleans. She'd have to move away."

For a long moment both girls were silent. Marie-Grace's thoughts whirled. Was it possible that Aunt Océane's singing career could be ruined by cruel gossip?

What if Aunt Océane and Uncle Luc had to move away? she thought. *I'd never see them—and*

Cécile and I would never see each other at music lessons, either.

The idea was too awful to imagine. Marie-Grace picked up her sewing and began stitching so quickly that the crisp white fabric crinkled in her hands. "We have to stop people from saying terrible things about Aunt Océane."

"How?"

Marie-Grace thought hard as she stitched. She took out pins as she completed each section and jabbed them into the pincushion.

Cécile stood up and began to pace back and forth in front of the large windows. Then she turned to Marie-Grace. "Last week, one of my maman's gold earrings broke. So she took it off and put it on the table in the parlor. When she went back to get it, it was gone. Maman asked everyone in our family—even my little cousin, René—if we'd picked up her earring. We all said no. Then she asked the maid who cleans the parlor, and she said no, too. But Maman thought the maid might not be telling the truth." Cécile paused.

"What happened?" asked Marie-Grace, looking up from her sewing.

"I found out who the thief was!" Cécile said triumphantly.

"Who?"

"My parrot, Cochon! He likes shiny things, and he must have flown down from his perch and picked it up. I found the earring hidden in a corner of his cage. A coin was there, too! Maman was very sorry she'd ever suspected the maid."

"Oh," said Marie-Grace, disappointed. She went back to her stitching. *How does that help us?* she wondered as she slipped the needle through layers of fabric. Cécile's parrot certainly hadn't taken the crown.

"Don't you see?" Cécile continued. "We know that Madame Océane didn't take the crown—but maybe the person who did is someone no one else has suspected."

Marie-Grace paused for a moment, her needle poised in the air. "Maybe," she agreed. She began to feel a bit more hopeful.

"And the only way we'll be able to stop people gossiping about Madame Océane is if we find out who really *did* steal the crown," Cécile continued.

"Yes, but how? It could have been anyone."

Cécile shook her head. "It wasn't just anyone." She walked over to the wardrobe and studied it for a moment. "Whoever took the crown had to have known that it was in this wardrobe."

"*We* were here when Aunt Océane put the crown away," Marie-Grace said slowly, and then she froze, her needle still in the air, as she understood what Cécile was saying. She set her sewing down on the table. "The *thief* must have been here then, too!" She realized that whoever the thief was, he or she had almost surely been in that very room with them. The thief had pretended to be a friend but perhaps even then was planning to steal the crown. Marie-Grace felt a rush of fear.

"We have to remember everyone who was here," said Cécile with determination. She found a piece of paper on Aunt Océane's desk. "Would your aunt mind if I used this?"

"I don't think so," said Marie-Grace. "Why do you need it?"

"You'll see." Cécile took a pencil and started drawing. A few minutes later she showed Marie-Grace a sketch of the studio, with the antique wardrobe in the center of the wall closest to the door.

"We were both here," said Cécile, pointing to the drawing. "And Madame Océane was here."

"Let's use pins," suggested Marie-Grace.

She and Cécile put pins in the paper to show where people had been standing. The girls placed pins for themselves and Aunt Océane, and for the opera company members who had come in: Mr. Foxcroft, Miss Bell, Mr. DiCarlo, and Mr. Taylor. To keep track of which pin was which, Cécile wrote names on one side of the sketch and then drew arrows to the pins.

"Miss Bell's maid was here, too," recalled Cécile, her pencil poised in her hand. "What's her name?"

"Greta—and she's not very nice to Aunt Océane," said Marie-Grace, sticking in a pin for Greta with extra force.

"Was there anyone else?" Cécile asked. She tapped the pencil on the table.

Marie-Grace stared at the pins. She realized who they reminded her of. "Ida was here. She was pinning Aunt Océane's dress." Marie-Grace put in one more pin for the seamstress.

"That's everyone," said Cécile, adding Ida's name. "Now, I guess we can take out some pins and cross out the names, too, because we know the thief wasn't Madame Océane or one of us."

That left pins for Mr. Foxcroft, Miss Bell, Mr. DiCarlo, Mr. Taylor, Greta, and Ida. "It doesn't make sense that Miss Bell would have taken her own crown," said Marie-Grace. She removed one more pin.

Five pins remained. Marie-Grace stared at the paper. "Why would *any* of those people have taken the crown?"

"The thief must be someone who doesn't want Miss Bell to play the role of queen," Cécile said thoughtfully. "Since the crown isn't really valuable, I can't think of any other reason for someone to take it."

"But if Miss Bell quit, it would only help Aunt Océane, and we know *she* didn't take the crown," Marie-Grace reminded her.

"Could the thief have believed the diamonds were real?" Cécile wondered aloud. Then she shook her head. "No, everyone in the opera company must have known the diamonds were fake."

"Yes," Marie-Grace agreed. "Besides, if the crown *had* been real, it would've been locked away in a safe—not put on a wardrobe shelf." Then she realized something. "Oh no!" she exclaimed, her hand flying to her mouth.

"What?"

"Aunt Océane locked the wardrobe before she and Ida left the room," Marie-Grace said slowly. "The door was locked when I came back to get the crown, too. So the thief must have unlocked the wardrobe to take the crown out—and then locked it again."

"So?"

"Only Ida was here when Aunt Océane put away the key!" Marie-Grace stared down at the piece of paper. "Everyone else had already left. So either the thief just guessed where the key was—"

"Or it was Ida!" Cécile concluded. For a moment, neither girl spoke. It was frightening to think that someone they knew could really be a thief.

Marie-Grace knew that everyone respected Ida—and that she was Aunt Océane's friend, too. But what if Aunt Océane had been wrong to trust the seamstress?

Cécile got up and started to pace the room again. "I don't think that Ida *could* be the thief. She's one of the best seamstresses in New Orleans. Everyone says her dresses are *merveilleux*! She's very successful. Why would she steal a fake crown?"

Marie-Grace thought hard. "Ida wasn't here when Miss Bell said the crown was fake," she said after a moment. "She might have thought the diamonds were real. And she *has* been acting strange lately." Marie-Grace told Cécile how she'd overheard Ida talking with Aunt Océane in the studio. "It sounded as if Ida didn't want anyone to know she was leaving. And today when Janie and I wanted to search the sewing room, Ida wouldn't even let us in."

"That *is* strange," said Cécile slowly. She was standing by the window and peering out at the street below. "Look," she said to Marie-Grace. "Isn't that Ida?"

Marie-Grace hurried to the window. The drizzle was heavy now, and a mist had settled. From the upper-story window, it was hard to make out figures clearly. Yet among the people strolling outside, Marie-Grace saw a slender woman carrying a basket. The woman held her head high, but she walked with a slight limp, and she was leaving the Royal Music Hall.

"I'm sure it's her," said Marie-Grace. She turned to Cécile. "What if she's leaving for good? She could have the crown with her right now!"

"We don't know that for sure," said Cécile. "But let's see where she's going." She grabbed her cloak.

Marie-Grace took the drawing of the room, which listed all their suspects, and stuffed it under the table so that no one would see it. Then she and Cécile rushed downstairs and slipped out the front entrance. As they threaded their way past the people lined up to buy tickets, Marie-Grace looked for Ida. She saw that the seamstress was already across the street.

Marie-Grace and Cécile had to pause at the edge of the banquette as they waited for a chance to cross the busy avenue. Carriages and delivery wagons rumbled by. As soon as there was a break in the traffic, the girls ran across the street, their shoes sliding in the mud. Marie-Grace scanned the crowded sidewalk. She didn't see Ida. "Where did she go?" she asked Cécile.

"In there," said Cécile. She pointed to the cemetery by the church. It was an old grave-yard surrounded by a wrought-iron fence and tall trees. A groundskeeper was standing by the arched gate, but the gate was open.

"In there?" echoed Marie-Grace. The cemetery stretched ahead, cold and cheerless in the gray drizzle. Everything she'd heard about the ghost came rushing back to her, and she felt fear envelop her like the mist. *What if the ghost is there, waiting for us?*

Cécile seemed to read her thoughts. "We'll be together," she reminded Marie-Grace.

Marie-Grace thought of Aunt Océane—and the terrible things people were saying about her. She squared her shoulders. "Let's go."

"No, but..." Marie-Grace ran and found a twig from one of the trees that rimmed the graveyard. "Will this help?"

"I think so." There was a pause. Then Cécile stepped back and held out a piece of paper folded like an envelope. "Here it is!"

Together, the girls examined the paper. The outside was blank except for a small drawing of a flower in one corner. Inside was a message written in ink: *I am bringing money. Do not give up hope.*

"'I'm bringing money,'" Marie-Grace repeated slowly. The paper shook in her hands as she read the words again. The meaning seemed all too clear. "Ida must have sold the crown for money," she whispered.

Cécile tilted her head, studying the note. "But we don't know for sure that the message is from Ida. Maybe someone else left it here. Look, it isn't signed." Below the message, Marie-Grace saw that there was no name, only a curious oval shape with a dot in the middle.

"Maybe," Marie-Grace admitted. "But Ida

was here." She pointed to the oval shape. "What do you think that means?"

Before Cécile could answer, the clanging of a bell resounded through the mist.

"We'd better go," said Marie-Grace. She was about to leave when she noticed that they had accidentally kicked the bouquet aside. Marie-Grace bent to straighten it.

Then she saw the name engraved on the tomb:

Angélique Beaupré
1810–1844

Marie-Grace dropped the flowers. She felt a cold wave of fear. *Angélique!* That was the name of the singer who had died ten years ago. *Could this be the ghost's grave?*

The bell rang again, the noise echoing in the silent cemetery.

"Allons-y!" Cécile urged. "Hurry!"

Marie-Grace nodded, too scared to speak. She and Cécile ran through the gate just as the bell rang for the third time. They paused at the street only long enough to find a place to cross. Then they rushed to the Royal Music Hall, racing up the steps and arriving breathless at the front entrance.

As they entered the lobby, Marie-Grace told Cécile, "We need to talk with Louis!"

Cécile looked puzzled. "Why?"

Before Marie-Grace could answer, she heard the voices of Mr. Foxcroft and Mr. Taylor. They were arguing loudly as they came down the hall from the back of the building, and they were headed right toward the girls.

"You shouldn't have lied," Mr. Taylor was telling the director. His usual turtle-like shyness was gone. Now he sounded fiercely determined.

There was no way to avoid passing the men without turning around. Keeping her head down, Marie-Grace walked quickly, fixing her eyes on the marble floor and hoping that she and Cécile could slip through the lobby without anyone asking where they'd been.

"I saw the new crown that was just delivered," Mr. Taylor continued. He wasn't stammering at all now. "It's nothing like the one that was stolen. It's a cheap copy, and Miss Bell will feel foolish wearing it. You should have told her the truth from the beginning. And if you don't warn her, I'll tell her myself."

"You're only saying that because you're in love with Miss Bell—you'd do anything to get her to notice you!" Mr. Foxcroft shot back. "You know I can't afford an expensive copy. You'd better not say a word, or you'll lose your job."

Poor Mr. Taylor, thought Marie-Grace, still staring down at the floor. *He's in love with Miss Bell, but she doesn't even notice him.*

Then she heard Mr. DiCarlo's booming voice. She peered up. "What are you two arguing about out here?" Mr. DiCarlo demanded as he joined the other men.

Before answering, Mr. Foxcroft looked

around. For the first time he seemed to notice Marie-Grace and Cécile. "You there, girl in the blue dress—Mary!"

"Her name is Marie-Grace," Mr. Taylor corrected him sharply.

With a sinking heart, Marie-Grace paused. There was no escaping now. She looked up at the director. "Yes, sir?"

"Tell your aunt that we're starting rehearsal immediately after dinner," Mr. Foxcroft ordered. He ran his gloved hand through his white hair. "Tell her to be on time."

Of course Aunt Océane will be on time, thought Marie-Grace. But all she said was "Yes, sir," as she and Cécile hurried past.

As soon as the men were out of earshot, Marie-Grace whispered to Cécile what she'd seen engraved on the tomb—and who she suspected might be buried there.

Cécile whispered, "Could it really be the ghost's tomb?"

"Maybe Louis can tell us."

The girls found the doorman at the back

entrance, packing up his bag for the evening. "Louis," Marie-Grace asked breathlessly, "was the singer who died here named Angélique Beaupré?"

"Beaupré," repeated Louis. He stroked his chin as he thought for a moment. "Yes, now I remember—that was her name. Madame Angélique Beaupré. Why do you ask?"

"We just saw her grave in the cemetery," said Cécile. "And someone left a message there."

"You girls should not go to the cemetery by yourselves," Louis reprimanded them. "It is too dangerous." He picked up his bag. "But the dangers in the cemetery are from pickpockets and thieves, not from the dead. Just because there was a message on a grave, it doesn't mean that a ghost has come to haunt us."

What **does** it mean? Marie-Grace wondered.

10
THE SECRET MESSAGE

As soon as Marie-Grace and Cécile were back in Aunt Océane's studio, Cécile pulled the folded paper from her pocket. The drawing on the front had been smudged by rain, but it was clearly a flower.

"Do you think it has something to do with the flowers on the grave?" asked Marie-Grace.

"There's no address on the paper," Cécile said thoughtfully. "Maybe the flower stands for a person's name. I know a girl named Violet— she sometimes draws pictures of violets by her name."

"You're right!" said Marie-Grace. She studied the flower again. "It looks like a rose. Maybe the note is for someone named Rose or Rosemary or something like that. But why not just write the name?"

"I don't know," said Cécile. She unfolded the paper and set it on the table. "And what about this?" she said, pointing to the oval marking. "It's shaped like an egg, but there's that dot in the middle of it."

Marie-Grace squinted at the shape. "It looks almost like an eye."

As soon as the words were out of her mouth, she had an idea. She looked at Cécile, and together they both said, "Eye for 'Ida'!"

"So Ida wrote someone a note saying that she's going to bring money soon and not to give up hope." Cécile carefully smoothed out the paper.

"Then Ida *did* steal the crown," Marie-Grace concluded. She felt a lump of sadness in her throat. Even though she'd suspected it before, it was hard to think of the talented seamstress as a thief.

Cécile seemed to feel the same way. "We don't know for sure that this note has anything to do with the crown," she cautioned. She thought for a moment. "And why did Ida leave it at a grave? It doesn't make sense."

"Unless Ida has some sort of secret—" suggested Marie-Grace. Before she could say more, footsteps clicked in the hallway. Cécile whisked the note into her pocket.

A moment later, the door opened and Aunt Océane greeted them. "Cécile, I didn't know you were here! And Marie-Grace, I've been so busy, I've hardly seen you." She sank down into a chair at the table and rested her head on her hands. "We must have rehearsed that last act a dozen times."

Marie-Grace gave her aunt the message from Mr. Foxcroft. "He said that rehearsal will start again just after dinner." She decided not to mention the director's remark about being on time.

"Oh, yes, dinner," said her aunt with a sigh. "I'm so tired, I'm not really hungry."

Cécile brightened. "I almost forgot—I have something for you!" She grabbed the basket that she'd brought from home. "Our cook, Mathilde, loves opera. She wanted you to have plenty of good food while you practice."

Cécile started pulling treats out of the basket. There were thick sandwiches on crusty French bread, a glazed cake, and a large tin of pecan pralines.

"What a thoughtful gift!" said Océane, taking off her gloves and sampling one praline and then a second. "Mmm. Délicieux!"

They each had a sandwich, and then Marie-Grace found a platter for the cake.

"Madame, you must try Mathilde's lemon cake," Cécile urged. "It is the best in New Orleans." The smell of tart lemons filled the room as Cécile cut slices for each of them.

Marie-Grace savored every bite of her cake. She hadn't realized how hungry she was until she'd finished the last crumb. Aunt Océane finished her slice, too, and then she poured tea for everyone.

"Cécile, that was wonderful! Please thank Mathilde for me—it was so kind of her to think of us." Aunt Océane sat back down at the table with her cup of steaming tea. Her cheeks were pink again, and she was smiling. "Now, tell me, what have you girls been doing? I didn't see you in the theater."

Marie-Grace and Cécile exchanged a glance. Then Marie-Grace took a deep breath. She knew it was time to tell her aunt their suspicions about Ida.

Aunt Océane listened as Marie-Grace and Cécile explained how they had followed the seamstress. "Oh dear!" Aunt Océane murmured when Marie-Grace told her about the note that they had discovered at the tomb. "You took it with you?" she asked, frowning.

"Yes," said Cécile. She pulled the paper from her pocket and showed it to Aunt Océane. "We think it's a secret message."

To Marie-Grace's surprise, her aunt barely glanced at the paper. "I don't want to read it," she said. Her teacup and saucer rattled as she set them down on the table. "It's Ida's personal note. You girls should not have opened it."

Cécile quickly refolded the paper, and Marie-Grace's face burned with embarrassment.

When Aunt Océane spoke again, her voice was calm. "I want to thank you girls for trying to help," she said. "I believe someone did steal that crown from my wardrobe, and I don't know who it was. But I'm sure it wasn't Ida."

Aunt Océane explained that she and Ida had both arrived at the Royal Music Hall at the same time, more than a year and a half ago. Since they were both far from home, the two young women had become friends. Then, during last summer's terrible yellow fever epidemic, they had worked together to help the sick—until Aunt Océane had become sick herself.

"Ida is one of the bravest, most hardworking people I've ever known," said Aunt Océane. Her blue eyes looked earnestly at Marie-Grace and Cécile. "I know she would never, ever steal."

"Oh!" said Marie-Grace, clenching her napkin in her lap. She now felt foolish for having suspected Ida.

Cécile spoke up. "But Madame, why did Ida leave such a strange note?"

Instead of answering right away, Aunt Océane stood up and poured more tea for everyone. "I trust you girls, and I know that you will do the right thing," she said at last. "So, since you've already learned some of the secret, I will tell you the rest."

Aunt Océane still trusts us, thought Marie-Grace, relieved.

Her aunt sat back down at the table. Then she asked Marie-Grace and Cécile to imagine what would have happened if Ida had been separated from her family for a long time.

"She would miss them," said Cécile.

"A lot," added Marie-Grace.

"*Oui,*" Aunt Océane agreed. Then she said slowly, "What if Ida found out that her little sister was a slave at a plantation not too far from here?" Aunt Océane looked at the girls. "Don't you think Ida would want to help her sister and buy her freedom if she possibly could?"

Marie-Grace nodded. Her father had always

taught her that slavery was wrong—and that everyone deserved to be free. "Yes," she said.

"My *grand-père* was once a slave, and he risked his life to become free," said Cécile, her face very serious. "He said he'd do anything to prevent his family from being slaves."

Aunt Océane said quietly, "And what if Ida had to give her sister a message but could not send a letter by mail?"

Marie-Grace considered this. She knew that slaves were not allowed to learn to read or write—although some slaves learned anyway.

"Maybe she'd find someone who could give messages to her sister without anyone finding out," Cécile suggested.

"Yes," said Aunt Océane. "But she'd have to be very careful, wouldn't she? There could be no names on the message, in case it fell into the wrong hands. A slave who receives or sends messages may be seriously punished."

No wonder the note didn't have an address and was signed with a picture instead of a name, Marie-Grace thought.

She imagined how lonely it would be not to get letters or messages from family and friends far away. She looked forward to Papa's notes when he was away, and she remembered how happy Aunt Océane had been when she'd received Uncle Luc's letter. Even homesick Janie could send a letter back to England if she wanted to. But Ida's sister couldn't write to anyone.

Do not give up hope, Ida's note had said. Now those words made sense to Marie-Grace. "I hope Ida can help her sister."

"I hope so, too," said Aunt Océane. "It can be hard to buy a slave's freedom, but in this case, it seems possible. Things could still go wrong, though, and it may be dangerous. So we mustn't tell anyone about Ida's plan until her sister is free and they are both safe."

Marie-Grace and Cécile promised they would keep Ida's secret.

"It's important that you return that note to Ida right away," added Aunt Océane. She stood up and gathered her music. "I must get back to the theater."

Aunt Océane headed for the door, but then she paused. "And girls, please do not worry about me. I know some people are saying bad things. But I've done nothing wrong. So we must all be brave."

"We will be, Madame," agreed Cécile.

Marie-Grace nodded, too. But as her aunt left the room, she didn't feel brave. She glanced at the wardrobe. *Someone came in here and stole the crown. How are we ever going to find the thief?*

Cécile's voice broke in on her thoughts. "We'd better take this to Ida," she said, putting the note in her pocket.

Together, Marie-Grace and Cécile climbed the stairway to the top floor and knocked on the door to the sewing room.

Ida opened the door just enough for a sliver of light to shine into the hall. "Yes?" she inquired. She was dressed in her bonnet and cloak, as if she was preparing to go out again.

"We have something for you," said Cécile. She held out the note.

Ida glanced at the paper. Then she stepped back, her mouth in a tight line. "You'd better come in," she said.

As they entered, Marie-Grace's eyes were drawn to the table near the window. Aunt Océane's brilliant blue satin gown was carefully laid out there. Alongside it was a dress made of silver satin, lavishly trimmed with lace. *That must be Miss Bell's costume*, thought Marie-Grace. Both dresses were finished and pressed. Their elegant skirts were so full that they took up the width of the table.

All the sewing supplies had been packed up and the room straightened. The only thing out of place was a large washbasin in the middle of the floor. Water leaking from the roof dripped into the tin basin.

Ida drew her cloak around herself and listened in silence as both girls apologized for having followed her into the cemetery.

"We're very sorry," Marie-Grace concluded.

She stared at the floor. "We never should have suspected you of stealing the crown."

"Of course I wouldn't steal," Ida said indignantly. "I've worked hard for every penny I've earned."

"Madame Océane told us about your sister, and we promise we won't tell anyone," said Cécile. She glanced around the room. "Are you leaving soon?"

Ida nodded. "I'm going tonight. I've finished all the costumes I agreed to make." She gestured toward the satin dresses that shimmered in the gaslight. "They're the most beautiful dresses I've ever sewed—I'm sorry I won't get to see them onstage. I've put so much work into them, and I want the opera to be a success." Her brows drew together. "Why on earth did you ever think that I took the crown?"

"Because you were there when Madame Océane locked it away. You saw her hide the key on top of the wardrobe," Cécile explained.

"And the wardrobe is too high for anyone to see over the carving at the top. I had to get a footstool to reach the key," Marie-Grace added. "You were the only person besides us who would have known the key was there."

Ida tilted her head, as if thinking. "The scroll decorates just the front of the wardrobe," she pointed out with an artist's eye for detail. "Perhaps a tall person could have looked from the *side* of the wardrobe and seen the key on top."

Marie-Grace drew in her breath. She hadn't considered that possibility.

"You should go now," said Ida, motioning the girls toward the door.

Marie-Grace said good-bye, but Cécile lingered. "Would you tell us why you left the flowers and note on the tomb of Angélique Beaupré? Is Angélique's ghost really haunting the opera?"

"The flowers are only a sign that a note is there to be picked up," said Ida. "I don't know anything about Angélique."

Cécile explained that Angélique was the singer who had died at the Royal Music Hall ten years earlier, just before opening night of *The Crown Diamonds*.

"Some people are saying that Angélique doesn't want anyone to perform the opera here," Marie-Grace added. "They say that she took the crown to cause trouble for Mr. Foxcroft's company. And Janie saw Angélique's ghost coming from the cemetery at night."

Ida shook her head. "I've heard rumors about a ghost, but I didn't know it was said to be Angélique. I only chose her tomb because the angel statue stands high above the other tombs. Someone who is looking for that grave can find it easily, even at night."

"But the gate is locked at night," said Marie-Grace. She remembered the iron fence that enclosed the cemetery. "How could anyone get in?"

"The fence is old, and a few pieces are bent," Ida explained with a half smile. "You don't have to be a ghost to slip through it. And the groundskeeper isn't there at night."

"But who will pick up the notes?" Marie-Grace asked.

"People I trust come to pick up the notes—I can't tell you who they are," said Ida in a low voice.

Then she opened the creaky door. "But I will tell you that I've been in the graveyard at night, and I have never seen a ghost there. I think the thief is someone who's right here among us. Someone who wants the opera to fail."

11
A DANGEROUS REHEARSAL

"Ida was right," said Marie-Grace as she studied the old wooden wardrobe in Aunt Océane's studio. The decorative scroll reached up high at the front of the wardrobe, but it was only at the front. The sides were plain.

She and Cécile walked around to one side. The wardrobe rose above their heads, but they realized that someone who was tall might have been able to see the key hidden on top.

Marie-Grace sat down at the table, still eyeing the wardrobe thoughtfully. "All we know now is that it wasn't a ghost who took the crown," she said. "It sounds as if the 'ghost' that Janie and Greta saw was really Ida."

"And we know Ida didn't steal the crown," said Cécile, sitting down next to her. "So we can take one more name off the list."

Marie-Grace reached under the table and pulled out Cécile's sketch of the room. Some of the pins were lopsided now, but the drawing was still labeled with the names of everyone who had been in the room. Cécile found a pencil and crossed off Ida's name.

The names left were Mr. Taylor, Mr. DiCarlo, Mr. Foxcroft, and Greta.

Looking at the wardrobe, the girls decided that Mr. Taylor was too short to have seen the key easily. "He would have had to stand on something to see the top," said Marie-Grace. "Besides, if Mr. Taylor really is in love with Miss Bell, why would he want to make her unhappy?"

Cécile put a question mark by Mr. Taylor's name. Then she studied the drawing. "Both Mr. DiCarlo and Mr. Foxcroft are tall," she said, pointing at their names with the pencil. "They could have seen the key. Greta's probably tall enough, too. Any of them could be the thief."

"But Mr. DiCarlo is in love with Miss Bell,

too," Marie-Grace objected. "And this is his first performance ever in America. I think it means a lot to him."

She stared at the names still on the list. "I can't see why Greta would want the opera to fail, either," she said. "She's loyal to Miss Bell—remember how upset she was when she saw Aunt Océane trying on the crown?"

Cécile's eyes lit up. "What about Greta's cousin, Janie? She misses England a lot. Janie might think that if she can stop the opera, they would all go home!"

"How would Janie have known where the key was?" Marie-Grace asked.

"She and Greta share a room," Cécile reminded her. "Maybe Greta told her where Madame Océane had put the crown." Cécile jumped up and grabbed the footstool. "If Janie had stood on this and looked for the key, she could have unlocked the wardrobe."

"I suppose it's possible," Marie-Grace agreed reluctantly.

Cécile sat back down at the table and

penciled "Janie" in light letters by Greta's name.

Marie-Grace tried to imagine the timid maid stealing the crown or putting the cat in Miss Bell's dressing room. She sighed. "I just can't picture Janie as a thief, though. She seems scared of everything."

"Then that leaves Mr. Foxcroft," said Cécile. She jabbed the pencil at his name for extra emphasis.

Marie-Grace considered the director carefully. "I don't like him," she admitted.

"I don't like him either," Cécile agreed. "And he lied to Miss Bell about the new crown."

Marie-Grace sat up straight. "He lied about something else, too," she said. She told Cécile how that morning, Mr. Foxcroft had said the opening night performance was sold out. "This afternoon, though, a sign outside the music hall said that tickets were still available. So opening night *wasn't* sold out."

"Then Mr. Foxcroft has lied twice," Cécile said. She drummed the pencil against the table. The noise echoed in the room like a tiny woodpecker. After a moment, she looked up at Marie-Grace. "Maybe Mr. Foxcroft has decided he doesn't want to put on the opera after all. Maybe it costs too much—he's always complaining about money. So he stole the crown hoping that Miss Bell would quit. Now he's blaming everyone else just so no one will suspect *him*."

"That might be it," Marie-Grace agreed excitedly. Yet she wasn't sure. The director had said that the opera company's reputation depended on the show's success. Would he really want to ruin it?

Looking down at the drawing, she considered the suspects—Mr. Taylor, Mr. Foxcroft, Mr. DiCarlo, Greta, and possibly Janie.

The thief has to be one of them, she thought. *But which one?*

There was a quiet knock on the door, and the girls jumped up. "Just a moment," called Marie-Grace. She quickly crossed the studio and hid the drawing in her satchel. Then she said, "Come in."

Cécile's maid entered and announced that it was time for Cécile to go home. Cécile told Marie-Grace that she couldn't be at the theater for opening night, but she and her whole family were going to attend the Friday performance. "I hope everything will be all right till then," she added.

As the girls said good-bye at the door, Cécile gave Marie-Grace a hug and whispered, "Good luck!"

"Thank you," said Marie-Grace, warmed as always by Cécile's friendship. *If only I knew what to do,* she thought.

As she lay in bed that night, Marie-Grace remembered Ida's words: "I think the thief is someone who's right here among us. Someone who wants the opera to fail."

Marie-Grace felt a chill. *After all Aunt Océane's hard work, the opera mustn't fail,* she thought. She wrapped herself tightly in her blanket before finally falling asleep.

When Marie-Grace awoke the next morning, her first thought was, *Today is the last day of rehearsals. We're so close now. I hope everything goes well.*

Downstairs, Louis handed her a note that had been delivered that morning. Marie-Grace opened it and read:

> *My patients are recovering, and I'll see you tomorrow for opening night.*

Marie-Grace held tight to the note as she walked through the greenroom. She passed several chorus members sitting at the long table. They were slumped in their chairs, hardly even talking. When Mr. Foxcroft walked in, they all looked worried.

The director glanced around the room, and then his eyes fell on Marie-Grace. "You there, Mary!" he barked. "I want you to go to the upper box seats and listen to the chorus rehearse. Tell me if you can hear everything. Can you do that?"

No one else seemed to be answering to "Mary," so Marie-Grace decided that the director must be talking to her. "Yes, sir," she said.

"Come with me," ordered Mr. Foxcroft, leading the way through the maze of ropes backstage. They stepped onto the stage, which was filled with scenery and crowded with performers preparing for the next act. It was noisy and confusing, but Marie-Grace listened carefully as Mr. Foxcroft pointed out where she should sit.

Following the director's instructions, she went down to the main floor of the theater. As she hurried past rows and rows of empty seats, Marie-Grace imagined what the theater would look like on opening night, when it would be filled with men in their best suits and ladies in fancy gowns.

She climbed the stairs and let herself into one of the small private boxes that overlooked the stage. The seats up here were expensive, and the private box boasted gold trim and a thick carpet. Marie-Grace sat down on a velvet-cushioned chair and surveyed the theater.

Everything looked different from this perch. The stage no longer seemed crowded and chaotic. She could see that it was decorated like a royal palace, and from this distance the scenery and props looked real.

The chorus began to sing, accompanied by the orchestra. Mr. Foxcroft directed them with extraordinary energy, swinging his baton as if he were casting a spell with a magic wand.

Marie-Grace's heart soared as she listened. She'd thought that the chorus sounded wonderful the first time she'd heard it, but now it was ten times better. The singers' voices blended together in perfect harmony. For a moment, Marie-Grace felt as if they were all singing just for her.

When the music ended, Mr. Foxcroft rested his baton. He looked up at Marie-Grace. "Could you hear the singers?" he called to her.

"Yes, sir," she called back. "Every word."

Mr. Foxcroft faced the chorus. "That was a bit better," he told them, and he sounded almost pleased.

Then he turned to the orchestra, and his voice rose to a bellow again. "You must play with more feeling! And the violins are off-key!" Mr. Foxcroft had the orchestra play the same passage several more times until he was satisfied.

The rest of the cast came onstage next. They had been ordered to rest their voices for the dress rehearsal, and they did not sing with full power. But even so, the mistakes began to multiply.

The orchestra kept playing the wrong notes, and Aunt Océane looked flustered when she had to begin her song again. *Poor Aunt Océane!* thought Marie-Grace, biting her lip.

Mr. DiCarlo was supposed to rehearse with Aunt Océane, but his strong voice sounded slightly off-key, and he confused two lines of the lyrics.

"Pay attention, Roberto!" Mr. Foxcroft shouted. "Do you want your first performance in America to be a disaster?"

Mr. DiCarlo's face turned red. "It's already a disaster, and it's all your fault!" he accused the director. Then he stormed off the stage.

Oh no! thought Marie-Grace, gripping the edge of the box. *I hope Mr. DiCarlo doesn't quit now—not when we're so close to opening night.*

Miss Bell hurried after the leading man. A moment later she returned by herself, looking upset.

Mr. Foxcroft ordered everyone to come onstage. Marie-Grace left the private box and went down to the stage, too. She stood at the edge of the group, across from Greta and Janie.

Mr. Foxcroft glared at the assembly. "This is a disgrace!" he declared. "How are we going to open tomorrow if we can't even finish a rehearsal? I've half a mind to cancel the show right now."

Marie-Grace glanced up and saw that Janie's eyes were bright with hope as she listened to the director. *Janie really would like the show to be canceled,* Marie-Grace realized with a shock.

As she looked at Janie standing next to Greta, Marie-Grace noticed that the cousins resembled each other. Janie was much younger and smaller, but both cousins had the same light brown hair and square jaw. Janie had always seemed timid, but Marie-Grace now wondered if she might be just as determined as her cousin. Had Cécile's theory been right? Could Janie be trying to stop the opera tour so that she could return home to England? Would she have gone as far as putting the cat in Miss Bell's dressing room—and stealing the crown?

Marie-Grace's mind was spinning as she looked at the other girl. *Maybe she is the thief!*

For several minutes, Mr. Foxcroft told the assembled singers and musicians everything that they'd been doing wrong. Finally he said, "You may take a rest now. Meet back here at one o'clock for the final dress rehearsal. And don't be late!"

As the cast and crew drifted off, Mr. Foxcroft spoke with Aunt Océane and Miss Bell at the front of the stage. Marie-Grace heard him say that he'd learned Ida had quit.

"Just what we need," the director complained. "A seamstress who runs off before the show!"

Aunt Océane assured the director that Ida had finished the costumes before she left and that the dresses were upstairs in the sewing room.

"Roberto and I saw my silver dress last night," added Miss Bell. She beamed. "That Ida is a genius! The costume she created is magnificent—I'm so looking forward to wearing it."

Aunt Océane and Miss Bell went backstage, and Marie-Grace went with them. Most of the cast had gathered in the greenroom. Cold meats, cheeses, and breads were set out on the table, along with a large cake studded with dried fruits and nuts.

"Have some fruitcake, ma'am," Greta urged Miss Bell anxiously. "You must keep up your strength. And my grandmother used to say it's good luck to eat fruitcake."

"Heaven knows, we could use some good luck!" said Miss Bell. "I really don't think I could stand having anything else go wrong." She took a slice of the cake, and other cast members did, too.

While everyone was talking, Marie-Grace noticed Janie slipping away from the group. She watched as Janie walked quickly down the long hall, and she remembered the look of relief that had crossed Janie's face when Mr. Foxcroft suggested canceling the show.

I'd better find out what Janie's doing, Marie-Grace thought. She hurried down the hall and into the lobby, her shoes pattering on the cold marble floor. She didn't see Janie in the lobby, so she continued up the stairs.

As she reached the second floor, she heard a door down the hall click shut. She guessed that Janie was climbing the narrow stairs to the top floor.

Marie-Grace was about to follow Janie up the stairs when she heard a muffled scream.

12
LAST CHANCE

Her heart pounding, Marie-Grace opened the door to the staircase. She almost collided with Janie, who was running down the stairs. Janie's face was white, and she looked terrified.

"What's wrong? Are you hurt?" Marie-Grace asked her.

"No! But the costumes in the sewing room—" Janie wailed. "They're, they're..." She started to sob.

Marie-Grace knew that something terrible must have happened to the beautiful dresses. Fighting back her own fear, she stepped into the stairway. "Let's go up there," she said to Janie. "You can show me what's wrong."

Janie shivered, but she followed Marie-Grace to the top floor. The door to the sewing room was half open. Marie-Grace forced herself to step inside.

Last night, the two elegant satin gowns had been carefully arranged on the table. Now they were both crammed into the large tin basin in the center of the room. Only the edges of the dresses' wide skirts dangled over the rim. Stepping closer, Marie-Grace saw that the gowns were soaking in dark water.

"The ghost of the prima donna did this!" Janie exclaimed. "She doesn't want us here." Wide-eyed, she looked around the room as if expecting the ghost to appear at any moment.

Marie-Grace glanced around the empty room uneasily. She reminded herself that the "ghost" Janie had seen had probably been Ida leaving messages in the cemetery. She took a deep breath. "I don't think a ghost did this," she told Janie. "I think it was a person."

And I think it's the same person who brought the cat into Miss Bell's dressing room and stole the crown, Marie-Grace thought. But seeing how horrified Janie was by the damaged costumes, she couldn't believe that the maid was responsible.

Janie looked at the soaking dresses. "Greta asked me to bring Miss Bell's costume down for the dress rehearsal. But Miss Bell can't possibly wear that." Janie wiped her eyes. "I guess— I guess I'd better tell Greta what's happened."

"No!" Marie-Grace burst out. She knew that as soon as Greta heard about the costumes, everyone else in the show would know, too. If Miss Bell learned that her beautiful new dress had been damaged, she was likely to quit. And then what would happen to Aunt Océane?

"First, let's take the dresses out of the water," Marie-Grace told Janie. "Maybe we can start drying them."

Marie-Grace pushed up her sleeves and reached into the dark water. She grabbed the silver costume first. When she'd gathered up all of the dripping material and squeezed out as much water as she could, she set the dress on the worktable. Then she stepped back, and her eyes widened. "Oh no!"

The gorgeous silver dress was not only soaking wet, it was streaked with blue. Marie-Grace realized that the water in the basin had been stained by the dye from Aunt Océane's blue dress.

Her heart sinking, Marie-Grace pulled the blue dress out and laid it next to the silver one.

Janie shook her head sadly as she looked at the dark blue stains on the silver dress. "That will never come out," she said.

"*What* will never come out?" demanded Greta. The girls turned and saw the maid striding into the sewing room.

Greta went pale when she saw Miss Bell's gown. Then she pointed her finger at Marie-Grace. "You did this, didn't you?" she said, her voice rising in anger. "Look at you—you're covered in blue dye!"

Marie-Grace glanced down. Her hands and arms were tinted blue from reaching into the water.

"No, Greta, you're wrong," Janie declared. She explained that she'd discovered the dresses and that Marie-Grace had come to help her.

At first, Greta didn't want to believe that

Marie-Grace wasn't to blame, but at last Janie convinced her. Greta stared down at the once-beautiful dress, now ruined. "I'll try to wash this," she said with grim determination. She touched the wet satin and then looked at her fingers. They were streaked with blue. "But the dye stains badly—how am I ever going to get it out?" She shook her head. "Who could have done this?"

Marie-Grace was asking herself the same question: *Who could it have been?* She wished Cécile were there with her. But Cécile wouldn't return to the Royal Music Hall until the day after the opening. That would be too late.

If I can't find out who did this, the show may not open at all, thought Marie-Grace.

Greta rolled up her sleeves and began gathering up the silver dress. As Marie-Grace moved a stray pin out of Greta's way, she thought of the pins that she and Cécile had used when they'd tried to figure out who had stolen the crown. The last time the girls had studied the pins, they'd thought that perhaps Janie or Greta was the thief. Now Marie-Grace felt sure that both maids were innocent. The only suspects left were Mr. Foxcroft and Mr. DiCarlo—and possibly Mr. Taylor.

Marie-Grace looked down at her own stained hands. She realized that whoever had crammed the costumes into the basin must have pushed them down into the water—so whichever of the men had done this had probably stained his hands, too. *If only I could see their hands,* she thought. *Then I'd know who it was.*

But she knew that Mr. Foxcroft and the two leading men often wore formal white gloves. How could she uncover the truth in time? Suddenly she had an idea.

"Miss Bell will be so upset when she finds out what's happened," Greta said as she hoisted the wet material from the table.

"Could you wait to tell her?" Marie-Grace asked urgently.

"She has to get ready for the dress rehearsal!" Greta protested. "And we'll have to find another dress for her to wear."

"If you could wait just a bit, I think we can find out who did this," said Marie-Grace, and she told Greta and Janie her idea.

At first they looked skeptical, but then Greta nodded. "It's worth a try, I suppose. But you'd better wear gloves, or your hands will give you away." Greta left the room and returned a few moments later with a pair of well-worn white gloves.

They were too big for Marie-Grace, but she put them on anyway. "Thank you," she said.

Greta smiled for the first time since Marie-Grace had met her. "You're welcome." She glanced at the dresses with a curt nod. "And I hope you find out who did this."

While Greta stayed to take care of the costumes, Marie-Grace and Janie went downstairs to Aunt Océane's studio. They found the basket of treats that Cécile had brought the day before. Marie-Grace was relieved to see that there were still lots of pralines left in the tin.

She carried the tin down to the hall of dressing rooms, with Janie following behind her.

The door to Mr. Foxcroft's office was open. Inside, Miss Bell, Mr. DiCarlo, Mr. Taylor, and Aunt Océane were sitting around the mahogany table. Marie-Grace paused near the door, gathering her courage.

"Maybe I should wait out here in the hall," Janie whispered.

"No, I need your help," Marie-Grace whispered back. "We must both try to look at everyone's hands."

"What if Mr. Foxcroft gets angry?" Janie asked anxiously.

"Don't worry," Marie-Grace said, even though her own heart was fluttering. "We'll be there together."

Taking a deep breath, Marie-Grace stepped through the doorway. The adults were talking among themselves, and she wondered how she could ever get their attention. But when she glanced at Aunt Océane, she remembered her aunt's words: "We must be brave."

I will be brave, she decided.

Marie-Grace smiled and announced loudly,

"My friend Cécile brought some delicious pralines for everyone." She showed them the tin. "Would you like one?"

Aunt Océane looked surprised, but she took off her gloves and helped herself to a praline. "They *are* delicious," she told the others. "Thank you, Marie-Grace."

Mr. Taylor wasn't wearing gloves, so when he reached for a praline, Marie-Grace could see his hands clearly. There was no trace of blue on them.

"And you, sir?" said Marie-Grace, offering Mr. Foxcroft the tin.

The director scowled at her.

Janie spoke up. "People say it's good luck to have a sweet before the show."

"In that case..." Mr. Foxcroft reached up.

"You'd better take off your gloves, sir," Marie-Grace told him hastily. "These pralines are a bit sticky."

He removed his gloves and grabbed a praline. Marie-Grace craned her neck to catch sight of the director's hands. She didn't see any blue stain on them. *Was I wrong to suspect Mr. Foxcroft?* she wondered.

Marie-Grace walked around the table to Miss Bell and Mr. DiCarlo, who were sitting side by side. She offered them the tin. The prima donna wasn't wearing gloves, and she daintily helped herself to a small praline. Her hands were unstained.

Marie-Grace asked Mr. DiCarlo, "Would you care for some, sir?" But the leading man didn't even look up.

"I'd better get dressed," said Mr. Taylor. He pushed his chair back from the table.

Marie-Grace looked over to Janie, who was still standing on the other side of the table. The two girls exchanged panicked glances. They hadn't found any clues, and they were running out of time. Any moment now, Miss Bell would be asking where Greta was.

Marie-Grace tried again. "Mr. DiCarlo," she said, "don't you want a praline?"

Mr. DiCarlo continued to ignore her. Marie-Grace felt her heart thudding in her ribs like a drum. *What if my plan fails?*

Then Miss Bell touched the leading man's arm. "Roberto, you must have a praline for good luck. Besides, they're delicious!"

The big man smiled at Miss Bell. Then, before Marie-Grace could say anything, he reached for the tin without taking off his gloves. But as he stretched out his arm, Marie-Grace caught her breath. A sliver of bare skin showed between his glove and his shirt cuff, and it was stained blue.

The tin of pralines shook in Marie-Grace's hand. *It was Mr. DiCarlo who ruined the dresses,* she thought. *He must be the thief!*

Miss Bell pushed her chair from the table. "It's time for me to get ready," she said. "I can't imagine what's become of my maid." The prima donna turned to Janie. "Would you find Greta and tell her I need my costumes?" It was more of an order than a question.

Janie hesitated for a moment. *She can't leave now!* thought Marie-Grace. *Didn't she see Mr. DiCarlo's arm?*

But Janie just said, "Yes, Miss Bell," and hurried away.

Marie-Grace looked around desperately. The cast members were all getting up from the table. She knew that the ruined costumes would be discovered soon. *It's up to me,* she realized, her mouth dry with fear. *If I don't say something now, I might not have another chance.*

13
COURAGE!

"Mr. Foxcroft..." Marie-Grace began.

The director turned his piercing eyes on her. Marie-Grace could feel everyone else at the table looking at her, too. But she continued, "I think I know who stole the diamond crown. It's the same person who ruined Miss Bell's new costume."

"My new costume—ruined?" echoed Miss Bell. She stood up.

"Who is responsible for these outrages?" Mr. Foxcroft thundered.

Marie-Grace held tight to the tin of pralines in her hands. She said, "It's Mr. DiCarlo."

Someone gasped, and a murmur of surprise spread through the room. The leading man was hunched over in his chair. Miss Bell elbowed him. "Roberto! Did you hear what she accused you of? Why don't you say something?"

Mr. DiCarlo threw an angry glance at Marie-Grace. "I don't know what you're talking about, you foolish child," he sputtered.

*He's a thief **and** a liar!* Marie-Grace thought angrily.

Just then, Greta stomped into the room, followed by Janie, who looked triumphant. *Janie didn't desert me,* Marie-Grace realized with relief. *She went to get help.*

Greta pointed at Mr. DiCarlo. "Is it true? Are you the one who's caused all this mischief?" she demanded. "Janie says there's a stain still on your arm."

Mr. DiCarlo looked around the room, as if searching for some way to escape. But all eyes were on him now, and the proof was on his arm. Staring down at the table, he finally admitted, "Yes, it's all true."

"Then there wasn't a ghost?" asked Janie. She didn't seem scared now. "It was you?"

Mr. DiCarlo nodded. Slowly he explained

that he'd learned about the prima donna who had died and had decided to use the ghost story to frighten Miss Bell. Mr. DiCarlo confessed that he had brought the cat into the dressing room and taken the crown, too. He said that he'd never meant to keep the crown forever. He had been hiding it in his hotel room and planned to "find" it later.

"And the beautiful dresses?" asked Greta, her hands on her hips. "You soaked them, didn't you?"

Mr. DiCarlo nodded. "I didn't want to hurt anyone. I just wanted to stop the opera."

"But for heaven's sake, *why*, Roberto?" asked Miss Bell. She sounded stunned, and her voice was barely louder than a whisper. "I don't understand!"

Mr. DiCarlo didn't say anything. *It's as if he didn't even hear the question,* thought Marie-Grace. Suddenly she remembered other times that Mr. DiCarlo had ignored people who spoke to him, and now she guessed why.

"Mr. DiCarlo, are you having trouble hearing?" she asked loudly.

The leading man looked up as if startled. Then he buried his face in his hands. "Yes," he admitted. "And of all the people in the world, why did this have to happen to me?"

He explained that during the voyage, he'd awakened one morning with a sore throat and ringing in his ears. "It's getting better, but I still can't hear well." He touched his throat. "I can't sing my best, either. I didn't want my first performance in America to be a failure."

"So that's why you stayed in your stateroom during the voyage!" exclaimed Mr. Foxcroft. "Why didn't you just tell me what the problem was, instead of lying, stealing, and causing trouble for everyone?"

Mr. DiCarlo shook his head. "I saw what happened to Henrietta when she became ill. She was left behind in Cuba. I was afraid that would happen to me."

He turned to Miss Bell. "I thought that if I could wait just a bit longer—until we got to St. Louis—then I could sing again as I always have." He put his hand on Miss Bell's arm and said pleadingly, "I was only thinking of you, Sylvia. I wanted our American debut to be a success. I wanted you to be proud of me."

Miss Bell shook off his hand. "If you'd only had the courage to tell me the truth, Roberto, I *would* have been proud of you! I would have fought for you to stay in the company, too. But you stole my crown, you lied to me, and you almost destroyed the show. You cared more about yourself than you cared about the opera." Tears began to roll down the prima donna's cheeks. "And you tried to blame others for what you did." She held a hand to her face dramatically. "I can't forgive you!"

With a sob, the prima donna turned away and rushed out. Greta scowled at Mr. DiCarlo, and then she and Janie followed Miss Bell out the door.

Mr. Foxcroft banged on the table. "Return that crown immediately, Mr. DiCarlo, or I'll turn you in to the police. And you are no longer leading man for this opera company. As far as I'm concerned, you can take the next ship back to England."

"I understand," Mr. DiCarlo said slowly. He rose to his feet and then bowed to Aunt Océane. "Madame, I'm terribly sorry that I caused you to suffer on my account. Before I leave, I will tell everyone in the cast the truth."

"Thank you, Mr. DiCarlo," Aunt Océane said with dignity. Then she gestured to Marie-Grace. "And I believe you owe my niece an apology, too."

To Marie-Grace's surprise, Mr. DiCarlo made a low bow in front of her. "I should not have called you a foolish girl," he admitted. "You discovered the truth—and I am the one who has been a fool."

The big, bearlike man looked heartbroken, and Marie-Grace's anger faded. She always felt sorry for anyone who was sick. "I hope you feel better," she told him. "My papa is a doctor, and he helped the passengers aboard the *Georgia.* Maybe a doctor could help you, too."

Mr. DiCarlo nodded grimly and left.

The office was silent for a moment. "Well," Mr. Foxcroft said finally. "At least there will be no more talk of ghosts." He turned to Mr. Taylor. "Can you take the role of leading man?"

Mr. Taylor blinked. "Yes, I suppose so." His voice was quiet, but then he added with determination, "I'm sure I can."

"Good!" said the director, pushing his chair back. "Then let's get to work."

The next night, Marie-Grace and her father watched the opening performance of the opera from an upper-tier box. The theater was packed with people eager to hear Miss Bell's American debut, and if Marie-Grace hadn't known better, she never would have guessed that there had been any problems. Aunt Océane's dress was now a lighter blue, but it was still lovely. Even Miss Bell's formerly silver dress, which Greta had dyed purple, looked properly queenlike.

Miss Bell charmed the audience with her dramatic acting and impressive high notes.

Mr. Taylor's strong voice rang out, and he sang without a hint of nervousness. It was as if he'd been destined to be a leading man all along.

Most important to Marie-Grace, Aunt Océane was magnificent. Her clear, beautiful voice filled the theater, and as she sang, her face glowed with happiness.

Nine days later, the sun was shining and the weather was warm as Marie-Grace arrived at the Royal Music Hall for her Saturday lesson. The music hall was quiet now that the opera company had left.

Marie-Grace found Aunt Océane and Cécile sitting at the table in the studio with cups of tea and a plate of crisp ginger cookies. They were carefully pasting reviews of the opera into a scrapbook. "This one calls the opera 'a crowning success'!" said Cécile, holding up an article.

"I will show these to Luc," said Aunt Océane, her eyes shining. She gave Marie-Grace tea in a delicate china cup and saucer painted with pink and white flowers. "I received a letter from him today. He's arriving home on Tuesday!"

Aunt Océane went over to her desk and took out a folded paper. She put it on the table. "I got this today, too."

Marie-Grace and Cécile quickly opened the paper and read the single line written inside: *Angels watched over us.*

Below the message there was a drawing of an eye. "It's from Ida," said Cécile.

"Does it mean that she and her sister are safe?" Marie-Grace asked eagerly.

Her aunt nodded. "Ida promised she'd send me a message when her sister, Flora, was free. They're moving to a city in the North where they have friends. I'll miss Ida, but I'm glad that she and Flora will be together."

Flora! thought Marie-Grace. The name sounded like "flower." *That must be why there was a flower picture on the note.*

Aunt Océane put away the message and returned to the table, smiling. "And there's more news, too—Luc and I are moving!"

The announcement startled Marie-Grace so much that she spilled her tea into her saucer. *Aunt Océane is going away!* she thought, horrified. "You're moving?" she echoed in dismay.

"Oui!" said her aunt brightly. "Luc has been worried about me having to travel so far to work, and so he found us a house that's near where you and your papa live, Marie-Grace. We'll be neighbors! And it has a pretty garden. You girls must come see it once we've settled in."

"I love gardens!" said Cécile.

"Me, too," said Marie-Grace. *Uncle Luc and Aunt Océane will soon be our neighbors,* she thought happily. She imagined strolling through the neighborhood with Aunt Océane and having tea in the garden with Cécile. Smiling, she told her aunt "I can hardly wait!"

LOOKING BACK

A PEEK INTO THE PAST

Across America, opera grew in popularity throughout the 1800s.

Many Americans today have never attended an opera. But when Marie-Grace was growing up, almost everybody in New Orleans was an opera fan. Children and adults regularly enjoyed thrilling performances that rivaled anything offered in New York or Europe, and huge crowds flocked to theaters to see the latest shows.

An *opera* is a play in which the words are set to music and sung. Performers sing with great power and emotion, their voices soaring to the highest notes and swooping to the lowest. Along with the glorious music, audiences enjoy the story and the elaborate costumes and stage sets.

Many operas that Marie-Grace might have seen are still performed today, including *The Crown Diamonds* by French composer Daniel Auber.

New Orleans was famous for having the finest opera productions and the most devoted audiences in the United States—and its magnificent theaters provided the perfect settings. The St. Charles Theater, in fact, was the largest, most extravagant theater in America. It had two

A scene in The Crown Diamonds *with Queen Catarin in the background*

tiers of balconies, a gallery above that, and luxurious boxes along the sides. The theater's huge chandelier weighed two tons!

The grand St. Charles Theater in New Orleans

The wealthy and fashionable filled the private boxes and plush balconies of the city's theaters. But everyone else came to the opera, too! Sailors, travelers, and families of shopkeepers, clerks, workmen, and farmers crowded into the cheaper seats. Free

In New Orleans, opera dr everyone—from the wealt like this family, to the po

people of color, like Cécile's family, sat in the upper gallery, and an area was set aside for slaves who had permission to attend. Everyone in the theater enthusiastically applauded good perfor- mances and shouted at bad ones!

New Orleans' theater companies, made up of local musicians and performers like Madame Océane, were excel- lent. When a New Orleans opera company toured the nation in the 1820s and 1830s, it outshone the opera companies of New York, Boston, and

Philadelphia and helped make opera more popular on the East Coast.

Opera companies from England, France, and Italy also toured America. Like Mr. Foxcroft's troupe in the story, they usually included one or two stars, some supporting performers and chorus members, and a director. Most used local orchestras and called on local professionals like Madame Océane to fill additional roles.

The leading European opera singers were the rock stars of their day—and nowhere were they more adored than in New Orleans. Newspapers ran stories announcing their tours, people jostled to buy tickets, and cheering crowds met the ships and escorted the performers to their hotel.

Despite the glamour and fame, life on the road was difficult and sometimes dangerous. In 1866, all fifty-seven members of a French opera company drowned in a storm

Opera star Adelina Patti got her start in the 1850s. Here, she is dressed as Rosina in the popular opera The Barber of Seville.

on the Atlantic Ocean. Once in America, companies traveled from city to city by steamboat or train, which involved the risks of explosions and crashes.

A deadly fire aboard a steamboat

Weather played havoc with schedules, too. In January 1856, an English troupe arrived in New Orleans nearly two weeks late because their steamboat had frozen into the Ohio River!

Just as in the story, illnesses such as colds, sore throats, fevers, and flu were common on the road. If a star fell ill, shows had to be canceled and travel delayed. With such difficulties, as well as the pressures of performing every night and being cooped up together constantly, it's not surprising that squabbles and spats often erupted in traveling companies.

For some Americans, travel wasn't just difficult, however—it was illegal. Slaves could not

Part of a letter written by a slave

travel without written permission from their owner. Laws also forbade slaves to learn to read and write. These laws made it very difficult for African Americans to keep in touch, so they found secret ways to get news to enslaved relatives and friends. Black sailors often carried messages—usually spoken, but sometimes written—as they traveled. Using symbols instead of names, as Ida did, could help prevent punishment if a message fell into the wrong hands.

No one knows whether a graveyard really was used as a drop-off point for secret messages, but a New Orleans cemetery would have been a good location. The aboveground marble tombs create many shadowy hiding places for a secret messenger—and a slip of paper!

GLOSSARY OF FRENCH WORDS

Allons-y! *(ah-lohn-zee)*—Let's go!

banquette *(bahn-ket)*—sidewalk

bien *(byehn)*—good

bonjour *(bohn-zhoor)*—hello

délicieux *(day-lee-see-yuh)*—delicious

fantastique *(fahn-tah-steek)*—wonderful, fantastic

grand-père *(grahn-pehr)*—grandfather, grandpa

madame *(mah-dahm)*—Mrs., ma'am

mademoiselle *(mahd-mwah-zel)*—Miss, young lady

Mais oui! *(may wee)*—Yes! But of course!

maman *(mah-mahn)*—mother, mama

merveilleux *(mehr-veh-yuh)*—marvelous, wonderful

mon Dieu *(mohn dyuh)*—good heavens; my God

monsieur *(muh-syuh)*—Mister, sir

non *(nohn)*—no

oui *(wee)*—yes

praline *(prah-leen)*—a rich, sweet treat made of pecans, brown sugar, and butter

une tortue *(ewn tor-tew)*—a turtle

How to Pronounce French Names

Angélique Beaupré *(ahn-zheh-leek bo-pray)*

Cécile *(say-seel)*

Cochon *(koh-shohn)*

Louis *(loo-ee)*

Luc Rousseau *(lewk roo-soh)*

Mathilde *(mah-tild)*

Océane Rousseau *(oh-say-ahn roo-soh)*

ABOUT THE AUTHOR

 Sarah Masters Buckey grew up in New Jersey, where her favorite hobbies were swimming in the summer, sledding in the winter, and reading all year round. She liked to read so much that whenever her parents packed their car for a vacation, her mother would include a grocery bag filled with library books just for her.

Ms. Buckey is the author of *Meet Marie-Grace, Marie-Grace and the Orphans,* and *Marie-Grace Makes a Difference,* as well as many mysteries. Several of her books have been nominated for national awards, and *The Light in the Cellar: A Molly Mystery* won an Agatha Award for best children's/young adult mystery.

She and her family now make their home in New Hampshire.